INCLUDE ME OUT

INCLUDE ME OUT

María Sonia Cristoff

Translated from the Spanish by
Katherine Silver

**TRANSIT
BOOKS**

Published by Transit Books
2301 Telegraph Avenue, Oakland, California 94612
www.transitbooks.org

Inclúyanme afuera
© María Sonia Cristoff, 2014
Originally published in Spanish by Mardulce
Translation copyright © Katherine Silver, 2020

First published in English translation by Transit Books in 2020

LIBRARY OF CONGRESS CONTROL NUMBER: 2019954071

DESIGN & TYPESETTING
Justin Carder

DISTRIBUTED BY
Consortium Book Sales & Distribution
(800) 283-3572 | cbsd.com

Printed in the United States of America

9 8 7 6 5 4 3 2 1

This work published within the framework of "Sur" Translation Support Program of the Ministry of Foreign Affairs and Worship of the Argentine Republic. *Obra editada en el marco del Programa "Sur" de Apoyo a las Traducciones del Ministerio de Relaciones Exteriores y Culto de la República Argentina*

This project is supported in part by an award from the National Endowment for the Arts.

NATIONAL ENDOWMENT for the ARTS
arts.gov

to M.T. Fournau

"I love fools' experiments. I am always making them.
Said Darwin."

Vanishing Point, David Markson

INCLUDE ME OUT

ONE

ON SOME DAYS she is able to follow the trajectory of a fly without anything or anybody getting in the way: its circular flight, the colors on its abdomen, the blur of its wingbeats, its buzzing, the precise instant it lands on a particular surface, its front legs engaged in a kind of frenetic prayer, its huge eyes, a moment of hesitation, its resolute—then idling—steps, its back legs poised to stalk, to flee, its desperate search for a way out, there, an inch away, a search Mara would assist were her circumstances different. On some days she manages to convince herself that she has learned to observe as if it were an act of simple confirmation. She sits in her museum guard chair and watches—silent, ecstatic, with no interruptions of any kind. For moments she believes that her experiment is working. Not always, but on some days she believes she's enjoying success. And if at one of those moments a visitor approaches to ask her a question about the museum or where the bathroom is or about the best local restaurants, she emulates the pieces in the exhibit, stares straight ahead at a tiny detail, turns a special quality of attention to how she is sitting, the tensing of her muscles, the expression on her face. To remain silent is also a discipline of the body, according to her manual of rhetoric.

• • •

A car drives by and the dust it kicks up covers her entirely.
A single car, all that dirt, an unlikely equation. She continues
walking. Three cows look at her and continue to chew their
cud. Why precisely those three, she wonders, they're not even
the closest ones. She would almost swear they were the same
ones that checked her out last Sunday, the one day she un-
failingly returns on foot. At five, when her shift is over, she
changes out of her uniform in one of the museum workrooms,
a little surreptitiously though she doesn't really know why, and
starts down the road that leads to the town where she lives.
It's an alternate road, used only by a few locals now that the
paved road follows a different route. It usually takes her three
hours to get home, sometimes a bit more. She wonders what
she'll do when winter comes and the days grow shorter; she
doesn't want to walk at night, doesn't want to pay extra attention to the dirt road or be twice as alert to the possibility of
an animal crossing in front of her or a car approaching, much
less ward off the unpredictable fear imprinted on any nocturnal
ambler. If there is something she does not wish to cultivate at
all it is a state of greater alertness. In fact, she has chosen this
routine of walking home at the end of the week in order to
make anything that might have happened over the previous
days evaporate, become vaguer and vaguer, more unstable, in-
offensive, nonexistent. She also doesn't want to have any ideas;
she doesn't need them. Much less memories. She wishes only
for the events of the week—at the museum, at home, on the
bus she takes every day other than Sunday, along this deserted
road that could be identical to any other road, during the in-

evitably gregarious lunches, in the garden that she will soon stake off, along the banks of the polluted river where she also sometimes walks—to vanish. All evaporated into air. And not because they torment her or anything of the sort, but because she wants them to be where they belong, where the truly forgettable belongs. Another car drives by at a paltry speed, which doesn't prevent it from spraying more dust on her clothes, her hair, her face. She rejoices mentally at those layers and layers of dirt making her ever blurrier, more like yet another mishap of the landscape.

• • •

She washes the leafy green vegetables with the utmost devotion, as if she were certain some new-generation plague or crucial clue were dwelling between the ribs and veins. She removes the ends and the singed edges. When she finishes making the salad, she realizes she's not hungry. She goes out to the garden, once again surprised by how big it is. She has to find someone to cut that grass, those weeds. She looks up at the star-studded sky. She must admit, this business of seeing the sky every day incorporates a whole different dimension into her perception of things, though she still would not know how to accurately define it. The only thing she knows is that sometimes it makes her a bit dizzy. The sensation is that everything has gone belly up and the sky is a basin into which she must, by force of habit, plunge. She returns to the kitchen, still not hungry, goes to the bathroom, thinks it's a good night to put away some things that are still in the few boxes left from her move. She sneaks like an intruder into the room where she stacked them. She drags one into the kitchen. It takes her a while, but she manages to organize her official papers into two piles. The other kind are more problematic: she doesn't even know why she brought them. To prevent anyone from finding them, she supposes, though the underlying megalomania of that amuses her in an odd way. Now she could eat, but the salad doesn't appeal to her. She decides to take a walk to the town center to see if she can find a place that's open. There's a breeze outside that feels good. She doesn't pass anybody on the first few blocks. Some dogs bark, though she doesn't know if in response to her passing. As she approaches the plaza, there are already some people sitting around tables at the two nearest bars, and there is already a line in front of a barn where, apparently, there's a dance. It's the first time since she moved to this town that it occurred to her to go out at night. She looks at her watch; it's past twelve. She listens to the music coming out of the open windows of the parked cars. The volume is turned way up, as if produced by equipment that is much more expensive than the cars they're playing in. She wonders what they're laughing about, what they're talking about, those who are in the cars and those who are in the two bars and those who are walking around the plaza. She's always wondered; this thing they call, in disco lingo, nightlife, has always been a mystery to her. And it was also a reason why her colleagues didn't trust her. Her former colleagues, from before, from then, from when her life consisted of traveling from place to place. How could she stay there in her hotel room, they would ask her, who was she with, what was her problem, what disease did she have. Any answer would seem to them more believable that her confession to a lack of interest. With time they believed her. Though not always, not all of them. There was that breakfast at the hotel in Cairo when someone, one of her booth partners who had been stammering particularly badly while interpreting at the conference the previous day, attacked her with rage and insults and with tears in her tired eyes, and at the end asserted that her lack of interest in going out at night was simply a strategy to remain clearheaded the following day and show up everybody else.

• • •

While eating her breakfast she stares at the kitchen shelves. For moments they look like pure geometric shapes. It's still early, which pleases her. One of the privileges of her new life is that she can get ready to go to work as if she were carrying out a ritual, with enough time to give proper weight to each step. The doorbell rings; she forgot that today they're delivering her weekly supply of vegetables. Ringo, the name of the farmer or what he wants to be called, apologizes for coming so early, expressing an abundance of remorse. When he brings in the order, he apologizes for asking for a glass of water and, at that very same instant, he sits down precisely where she had been sitting. Mara doesn't understand how the two or three cordial sentences they exchange once a week has led to this intimacy, and, moreover, she regrets having left her unfinished breakfast things on the table—she doesn't want witnesses, not even to that. Ringo looks dejected. She imagines him with a young wife and a newborn baby, who again last night didn't let them sleep. She pours him a glass of water and goes to the back door and opens it. A breeze enters. She stands there looking up at the sky, which at any hour of the day seems to her like a discovery.

Ringo stammers out a monologue. Based on what she manages to hear, there's a father who refuses to let Ringo study what he wants, a father who didn't abide by an agreement they made three years ago, when they came here, according to which he would become one more cog in the new family venture on the condition that when he finished high school, he would leave this town to go study whatever he wanted and not what his father had in mind, a father who now wears bombachas, those baggy peasant pants, and a beret, and is trying to convert him to his new religion. Remaining silent is a way of making others talk, Mara recalls from her manual of rhetoric. She closes the door and says to Ringo, lies to Ringo, that she has to be at work in an hour. He doesn't budge. He sits there staring at the two pits of the peaches he brought the week before and that she has just eaten. For Mara, the situation is already verging on the promiscuous. She tries to find another sentence that will push him to leave, but she only manages to take note of the setback her longstanding ability to guess the lives of others has just suffered: the selfless father of a young family ends up being a pampered young man with vocational problems. Just when she thought her powers of observation had entered their best phase. Who knows why, Ringo says, but at some point he thought that Mara would have advice for him, that she would have some ideas. Then, before he leaves, he picks up the two pits and sticks them in his pocket. From the window Mara sees that he appears to change his mind before he gets into his truck. He takes the two pits out of his pocket, throws them on the ground, and steps on them as if he wanted to crush them, taking his time with each one in turn. He uses his right foot for both.

• • •

From the *Notebook*:

The museum of Luján, today Udaondo, and its initial role as
a shield against the cosmopolitan version of the nation. As the
nation was approaching its first centenary, the menace disembarking from the ships was too great. On that shield: the gaucho
and the Indian. And, also, the recovery of its colonial heritage,
of *hispanismo*. All of this, empowered: modes of countering a
certain kind of novelty. The nation's fear of ships. Accumulation as a reactionary gesture. Udaondo, using his alliances with
political power and with donors, who were also connected to
political power. The inauguration of the Indian Room in 1926,
and the year before, the Gaucho Room. An embalmed Mataco
Indian in Udaondo's first museum. The wax gaucho and the
embalmed horse donated by Gustavo Barreto Muñiz. Already
vanquished on so many internal fronts, they could now join the
epic procession. Exhume the dead, exhume Indians and gauchos, like so many crucifixes to hold up against the threat of the
poor immigrants disembarking from the ships. Vanquish them,
as well. Design future shields on which the Indian, the gaucho,
the Criollo horse, and the hardworking gringo pioneer could
all live together. Shield and nation. The idea of the fatherland
and its incorrigible necrophilia. Accumulate the dead and the
leftovers. Güiraldes, who published *Don Segundo Sombra* a few
months after Gaucho Hall was inaugurated, was also embalmed.
Poor Güiraldes—so manipulated, so misinterpreted. His wid-
ow donated his collections to the museum. The importance
of wealthy women in the construction of Udaondo, in its ac-
cumulations. Accumulation and death. According to an article

in Natalio Botana's *Crítica* newspaper in 1926: "The museum is no longer a Museum, but rather a nest of absurdities that burn and freeze our blood." Udaondo biting his own tail.

(After María Élida Blasco, *Un museo para la colonia. El museo histórico y colonial de Luján* [A Museum for the Colony: The Historical and Colonial Museum of Luján], Rosario: Prohistoria Ediciones, 2011.)

• • •

Her boss calls her over when she sees her arrive. She tells her, invoking a camaraderie that catches Mara off guard, that she has something for her, she should come with her to her office. She tells her to make herself comfortable as she struggles to open a grim-looking Tupperware container, which resists her efforts. Finally she presents her with a piece of limp cake, like a dead fish. Mara mumbles a few sentences that combine a sorry and a thank you, both without any well-defined motive. But above all, her boss says, she wants to let her know how proud she is of her. Perhaps she shouldn't confess this, but she had her doubts the day she hired her, and now she realizes that they were unfounded, that sometimes in small towns people are too prejudiced against outsiders; she wanted Mara to know, in short, how happy she is to confirm that she made the right decision that day. Mara thanks her a couple of times, or more, with all the conviction she is capable of, before walking away down the hallway. She sits down in her chair with the greenish-colored Tupperware resting on her lap. She can't figure out if there was a museum anniversary, somebody's birthday, or a local holiday. She'll soon find out. One of the key protocols of the experiment she came to this town to carry out is to not ask questions. To speak the absolute minimum, and, above all, to never ask questions. One year, that's all. One year of practicing the art of remaining silent. She gets up, places the Tupperware on the chair, and starts to clean the room, as she does every Wednesday. As she sweeps, she reviews one of the ten kinds of silence as defined in her manual of rhetoric, the seventh: "The silence of consent consists of the approval we give to what we see or hear by limiting ourselves to paying favorable attention, which signals the importance we attribute to it, bearing witness—through a few external signs—that we consider it reasonable and that we approve of it." Her years as a simultaneous interpreter have equipped her with a prodigious memory, so she remembers even the punctuation.

• • •

Luisa's arm appears through the bars over one of the windows, open today because of the heat, and signals to Mara to hurry up. That's when she realizes it's already Friday. When she steps outside, the sun hits her like the blast from a furnace: intense, excessive. They walk the first few blocks to the restaurant without talking, which proves that she has found a true friend in this most unexpected of places. Luisa is wearing one of those dresses that Mara thinks of as hopeful, a wager on the coming weekend, a celebration of the calendar, and she eats with a voracity belied by her wiry body. She reports that they will soon get a raise, that she heard about it from management. If it weren't for the protocol Mara wrote for herself, which includes among its key items the reduction of any and all conversation to degree zero, she would ask her exactly how much the raise would be. Though she doesn't really care, the amount is probably negligible. That's not where she'll find the solution to not spending a single cent of her savings the entire year, another of her protocol items. Perhaps she should have rented her apartment instead of locking it up, but the less contact with her past life the better: another key item. After all, not having a single extra cent is the perfect excuse for not being able to do anything other than what she has laid out for these months, this year. It lends her experiment a pragmatic advantage. Luisa, it appears, has already moved on to another subject, because now she is talking about a couple who strolled through the gallery a few days ago, and, instead of looking at the candelabras, the paintings, the crucifixes, in other words, everything that was on display, they entered the room as if it really were a chapel— with reverence, she would say. The truth is that when Luisa saw them she felt kind of sorry for them because she knows that the entire museum is more like a stage set, and therefore less effective for achieving the result they were seeking, and that's why she approached them to tell them that just across the street is the church, but then she realized that something else was going on, that she, the girl, was masturbating her boyfriend or husband, her companion or whatever, with unbelievable skill: the only things moving were her fingers, not even her shoulder or her arm or even her forearm, not even her hand, just her fingers. She was using a very specific technique, like the one used by purse snatchers at bus stations and on crowded buses. She was on the verge of asking her about it but then reconsidered. Afterwards, as they were leaving, she wanted to make some witty comment, as if to signal her complicity, and then, who knows, maybe the girl would tell her how the hell she does it, but she couldn't think of anything to say, of how to ask. Too bad; she imagined several situations in which she'd love to use that technique. She'd swear that she, Mara, would have known what to say. That very night, while they were eating dinner, she told her aunt, but instead of thereby initiating a conversation on a subject that interested Luisa, that interests her, she had to listen to a keynote address on the aphrodisiacal nature of Catholic imagery. What can you expect from someone married to a Communist: that's what her mother would say every time she came to her with stories about her Aunt Honoria. At that time, her uncle The Red, as they used to call him in town, was still alive. As was her mother. Anyway, she also wanted to tell Mara that she signed their boss's birthday card for her. There wasn't much time to check with her, and anyway she was sure that Mara would have had issues with signing it, but she, who'd been working there for five years, not just a few months, knows all too well that something like that could cost someone their job. It turned out perfect, she would have to retrieve that card from somewhere to show her how well she can fake her signature, or what she imagines her signature must be. She also put in Mara's share for a gift. Mara agrees with her handling of the situation and tells her that she's wrong, she wouldn't have been able to think up a witty comment, either.

• • •

Mara arrives about ten minutes after the stipulated time. The person she is replacing looks at her with what appears to be excessive resentment, puts on a coat that is wholly unnecessary for noon on that boiling hot day, and leaves without saying goodbye. It's Saturday, and the first specimens of the cultural tourists who show up on weekends have arrived. That prospect, along with the heat, the sticky screeching heat, conspire against her ability to disengage from her surroundings, against her carrying out the exercises that usher her into detachment. The chair feels hard, uncomfortable, there's no question it will end up destroying her back, which has already been hurting for several days. Someone comes up to her to ask if it's really true that this man traveled more than twenty thousand kilometers pushing that wheelbarrow just to win a bet. She answers rudely, which makes her feel even worse: intense exchanges have no part in the protocol of her new life. She stands up and takes a turn around the room. Her back pain, she ascertains, lets up when she walks. She stops in front of Vasco's aforementioned wheelbarrow and confirms that, yes, the information as written is clear, this is not the source of the confusion. She keeps walking, slowly and in a zigzag. She stops in front of the two embalmed horses. She has never been that close to a horse, dead or alive or embalmed. To think that, like her, they traveled for years from place to place and are now motionless in this room. A paradoxical tribute. Truth is, she wouldn't have wanted any other kind. Her experiment in detachment arose, in fact, out of one of the most powerful forces in the world: saturation. She arrived in this town implacably fed up with what she had left behind. She would ask them, if they weren't horses, and if they weren't embalmed, if the same thing had happened to them. If they, like her, are examples of a wounded cosmopolitanism. Her head aches and feels heavy. She walks into the hallway for a glass of water so she can take a painkiller. The water in the water fountain is warm and the little plastic cups have disappeared. She figures she would waste more time if she tried to find out who is in charge of restocking them than if she left the museum and went to the kiosk to get a bottle of very cold water. Leaving the gallery completely unattended could become yet one more episode that would cost her the job, she thinks as she crosses the plaza.

• • •

From the *Notebook*:
In order to spy on an attractive and elusive neighbor, Xavier de Maistre, the character, identical to Xavier de Maistre, stands on the edge of the abyss, perched on his window sill, one leg on either side. It occurs to him that the nocturnal expedition around his room that he has decided to embark on could very well include a horseback ride—a ride on the back of one of those animals that always fascinated him, especially if they were inanimate. He rides on and on as his mind wanders over a broad array of subjects, memories, and considerations. An homage to Quixote? A fascination with horses, above all inanimate ones, of this alter ego who takes off on a voyage around his room for a second time. A character who goes into hiding after traveling widely. The first time, imposed on him by others: prison for having fought a duel; the second time, not: weary of the din of the world, he rents a small room where he knows nobody can find him. There he devotes himself to minute observations, philosophical digressions, art criticism, gossip, synthetic theories, eulogy, malice, memory, the unparalleled happiness of self-imposed reclusion. The parallel composition of an epis-

tolary poem, which is never published. Rage at the fatherland, war, Russian exile. The permanently mocking tone, a mocking tone that in de Maistre never flags. My temptation to imitate him in this other story of self-imposed exile, but there's an excess of mockery in our Pampas. Xavier de Maistre's saturation with discoveries and training and constant chatter. Saturation, saturation. Xavier de Maistre and his two expeditions around his room, which are set forth as manuals. Manuals to inspire stillness, observation, and silence. The quantity of things one can manage to hear, to think, if one remains still, still and alone, still and in silence. A different kind of mockery. A buzz.

(After Xavier de Maistre, *Voyage Around My Room* and *Nocturnal Expedition Around My Room*, New York: New Directions Publishing, 2016)

• • •

The lumbar moment—as she calls it when her vertebrae make contact with the back of a chair, never to move again, not for anybody or anything—gets better every day. She could assert without exaggeration that it is the most visible change in her new life. Before, she would sit down any old way, without thinking; now, she always pays attention no matter where that point of contact occurs, not only on the guard's chair in the room. Muteness is also the art of a still body, so says her manual of rhetoric. To that end, she has come all the way here in order to be still. Still and mute. Or, not exactly: remaining silent is important as a paradoxical speech act, so also says her manual. Mara is just now beginning to perceive the eloquence implicit in this business of remaining silent, and she enjoys it doubly, out of revenge, rage, and vengeance; she enjoys it because she is something like a survivor of a camp, a hospice, a ward, a fire, a conflagration, which in her case, took a discursive form, the form of the ritornello: *an interpreter can never, for any reason, remain silent.* In her booth, an interpreter can do anything: she can sneak a drink, pop pills, strip naked in front of the colleague she happens to be working with that day; she can plan an assault, a suicide, a brilliant heist that remains a mystery to the police for centuries; she can paint her nails or pull them out, say anything she wants, make mistakes, create a misunderstanding with fatal consequences, unleash a third world war, reveal an unspeakable secret; she can invent, mock, talk about what she dreamed the night before; she can shout, swear, facilitate an unexpected peace treaty, explode a distant bomb; she can make millions from that sentence they wrote down next to the number of a bank account that is impossible to trace; she can speak in dead languages like someone possessed; she can look at a photograph she would never show anybody and make comments about it; she can recite her favorite poet; she can read the headlines of a provincial newspaper; she can practice mnemonics; she can invent lines she doesn't know of a song she has just discovered; she can dictate her last will and testament; she can talk the way she talks to her dog or her lover in private, but never ever ever can she remain silent. She can even do what she did that day, but she can never remain silent.

• • •

Luisa walks up to her carrying a plate full of food that, she insists, Mara should eat. Mara really loves her—how is it possible to love someone after such a short time? Months is all, after having spent entire years without loving anybody, not a single person. Years. Mara looks at the abundance of sweet and savory items that supposedly she will eat. She picks something and chews slowly while Luisa starts to chat with one of the many women making the rounds at this celebration that she organized for her illustrious Aunt Honoria, whom she has lived with since she was a teenager, whom she chose to live with even though her parents weren't yet dead. There's nobody from the museum, or at least nobody Mara recognizes, except one of the librarians. The aunt does some kind of volunteer work at the library, if she remembers correctly. There's music playing in the background, which she also doesn't recognize. She would be able to sit there for hours if Luisa didn't keep looking at her and widening her eyes with a certain impatience. Okay, she'll have to relinquish her lumbar contact, her contemplation, in order to chat or at least pretend to: her muteness protocol provides several ways to get out of these situations. The most effective silence is the one that makes others speak, but in this case there's no need to make that effort at all. The group she approaches doesn't notice her presence and continues the conversation about the new minister and his misguided policies, what he was before and what he is now, what he really should have been before he wasn't, if memory serves, and so on. It's as if they'd learned the teachings of a religious cult and are now making plans to rid the temple of the Philistines. Then they continue with the story of somebody, which leads to the story of yet another somebody. Although she would like to go right back to her chair, Mara asks for the bathroom. Next to the office, they tell her. She starts down a narrow corridor lined with books on the spines of which, out of the corner of her eye, she manages to read a few names: Georgi Dimitrov, Einstein, Héctor Agosti, Paul Lafargue, Clara Zetkin, Victorio Codovila, José Díaz Ramos, Mariátegui, Marx, Engels, Ghioldi, Gramsci, Karl Kautsky, Antonio Labriola, Lenin, José Murillo, Leonardo Paso, Alcira de la Peña Aníbal Ponce. What did that uncle do with this hodgepodge, she wonders. There is something anachronistic about this office, something mawkish that families create when they refuse to get rid of the belongings of the dead. Maybe nobody ever enters, maybe it's a kind of mausoleum, and she is now committing an act of desecration. Maybe her silhouette will remain drawn in the air, as they say happens in Siberia when temperatures drop below thirty-five degrees below zero and the air turn into particles of frost. But no: on the desk are several stacks of handwritten pages and an appointment book open to this week. She looks at the pages before and after and sees that activities are planned through the last months of the year. She wonders if that book and that office-mausoleum function for Honoria as fantasies of control over the future and the past; she wonders what that aunt does in here. The seal of the museum library appears on several of the files surrounding the handwritten pages. And those pages are letters, all with different dates from the nineteen thirties. The script, in ink, is tiny and grows to an implausible extent when the signature of someone named Rosendo Leiva appears. She turns on a lamp and sits down to read. They are letters sent to Udaondo, the founder of the museum, letters in which Leiva says that he had a thousand gazettes printed, that someone wants to donate a sword, that someone else is demanding payment, that the trees are growing well, that the floats are now ready for the parade, that many, or few, people visited, that it rained a lot, or a little, that the shirt is ironed. Letter-reports, to tell the truth. "Yesterday there was a flood of people. Three trains full. From Bernal alone there were 1300. Forgive me for saying that not a single person failed to visit the Museum. There was a moment, between eleven and twelve o'clock, when all the rooms were well-nigh overflowing. When the bell rang, the sidewalk was darkened by people, and at one o'clock, when we opened, there was an avalanche." *A flood* and *was darkened* are underlined. Why not *overflowing* and *avalanche*, Mara wonders, and she sets out to investigate the system of underlining in other letters, but she stops when a light goes on. Luisa's aunt stares at her from the doorway. Only then does she realize that she is sitting on the edge of the chair, totally absorbed in that handwriting with those unforgettable phrases, her lumbar contact totally lost. *Un pelandrún*, Honoria proclaims, as if she were continuing a conversation, as if she had come up with the formula that would put an end to it. *Pelandrún*. A chill runs down Mara's spine: the torment has returned intact, the one she used to undergo when she would come upon a word that had been completely erased from her mental dictionary. During her last few months, mostly. To counteract the dread, she would assemble and write down at least three sentences using that word and stick them around the house in those inevitable places: the bathroom mirror, the door of the refrigerator, the jar of night cream. The word would come back, though at a steep price, because the implacable law of paradox decreed that employing methods from her student days made her feel old. She never felt so old as during that period of time, right before what happened, before her final act. *Un pelandrún*, Honoria insists, or so it seems to Mara, a middleman Udaondo left in charge of the museum while he was living in his palazzo in Buenos Aires and making off with all the glory. He gave speeches, talked to the press, posed for photographs, but the one who really ran the museum day in and day out was Leiva, and the poor man was so proud. Udaondo really knew how to manage things remotely. Give orders, that is, give orders remotely. If her husband ever found out that she was organizing the archives of a museum founded and run by a Catholic gentleman, a perpetrator of the colonial order, a collector of surplus value, he'd rise from his grave, Honoria says and sits down on a loveseat with very worn upholstery. But he'll see how, at the right moment, even from an archive in the provinces, the vindication he worked for until his last breath will emerge. It's just a matter of patience, she adds, now with her eyes closed. Mara doesn't know if she is talking to her or if she has turned into an interloper, intruding on one of many nocturnal dialogues in the office-mausoleum. She gets up to go, finally, to the bathroom. Luisa convinced her to organize this gathering, who knows why, Honoria adds, but the truth is that she can't wait for it to be over. If she were a guest like her, she says with her eyes still closed, she'd leave right now.

• • •

Imminent rain. She manages to see out the window how the street vendors with their carts full of trinkets flee the plaza and the stray dogs hurry to find shelter under an awning. The onset of storms has become one of her favorite spectacles, one of her new luxuries. She settles in to watch with the same anticipa-

tory pleasure she gets from the opening credits of a movie, but
two visitors enter right at that moment, two of those fashion-
able types who show up very infrequently in this museum. It's
incredible, incredible, he is saying without looking up from the
ground, as if searching there for a response. Leaving within a
month, everything's all arranged, the woman says. Buried alive:
he told her that's where it was heading, there's no other way
to look at it. Incredible, he continues. He looks about ten years
younger that the woman, and Mara considers how despairing it
must be to have a husband or a friend or a lover who is capable
of uttering a single predictable sentence in response to everything. They keep walking around the room, her room, the
Means of Transportation Room, but without seeing anything,
all the time actually circling around the story that, apparently,
features the woman's daughter as the main character. A daughter who has just announced that she will become a nun, and
not only that, a cloistered nun. Where could she have gotten
it, where, she says, folding herself into the repetitive prosody
of her companion while looking for something in her purse,
maybe the cigarette she would not be allowed to smoke inside. Mara suffers each time she sees the advent of one of those
situations that might require her to take repressive action as a
guard; truth is, she suffers from any side other than the con-
templative one. She's lying, lying to herself once again: she also
enjoys Wednesday cleanings, that intense flurry of mops and
disinfectants and special brooms that, like the Sunday walks,
help to empty her mind. The Zen of Pledge. That school the
priest wanted to send her to, she should have been removed
from there, the woman says before answering her cellphone,
which seems to be what she was rummaging around for. She

walks over to the window to talk. He tries to focus on a few of the objects, but he is obviously distracted, or rather worried, even upset. Mara can't figure out who he is, what connection he has with the future nun. Impossible to figure out if he's a stepbrother, a friend of her mother's who's known her since she was little, the new younger husband who's fallen in love a little with his stepdaughter. He looks distraught. And so fragile inside that jacket, which is so elegant and wrinkled. He goes over to the window, too, and stands there staring at what's going on in the plaza, or at nothing, how to know even though he's less than a meter, just centimeters, away from Mara's chair. The woman turns with a look on her face as if to say that she had to take the call, and it appears she's interrupting him, or at least that's how he reacts, as if he hadn't had time to hide something, his body tense. Maybe that's why, in order to shift attention elsewhere, he immediately points to the embalmed horses, which, Mara could swear, he hadn't looked at for even a split second during his first round. He asks the woman if she knew that they'd spent a week in Madison Square Garden, and he tells her that his great aunt has the femurs of one of these two horses, he doesn't remember which one, in her house. A famous silversmith made two lamps with them, which they didn't let him touch when he was a child and would go there to visit. How creepy, says she, who seems quite used to putting an end to topics of conversation. They keep walking in circles, as if this place were a waiting room and the doctor was taking his time with the results. Actually, no, as if the doctor had already said what he had to say but they hadn't fully taken it in and so they'd rather not go outside, they'd rather continue to wait, thinking that he was wrong, that the diagnosis belonged to another patient, the one in the other bed. Mara wonders if it could be true what she just heard; she thought that the bones remained inside embalmed bodies. She looks over at the horses, and this afternoon they seem to her to be in a worse state than ever, who knows why. The room grows darker because of the storm that has already started, and the visitors are still there, not moving either, like Mara, like the horses. Suddenly she has the impression that this woman and this man are in fact a couple of travelers who have lost their way and have come to the door of her house to ask for help, where Mara and her horses are happily watching the water pour down.

· · ·

From the *Notebook*:

Aimé Félix Tschiffely was one of those Europeans—Swiss by birth, English by choice—who came to Argentina to look for adventure or to flee from the continent at war, or for both reasons. Shortly after he arrived, he met up with his brother in a town on the Pampas in the province of Buenos Aires, then landed a position as an instructor at St. George's, but adventure still eluded him. As an ersatz educator, he felt asphyxiated. Octavio Peró, from *La Nación* newspaper, put him in touch with Emilio Solanet, the Criollo horses breeder who proposed creating a registered trademark, Argentinean and successful, out of that weary breed, so devalued in comparison to the "purebreds." A quid pro quo: Tschiffely would enjoy his quota of exotic adventures if he managed to ride from Buenos Aires to Washington, DC, with Mancha and Gato, two of Solanet's Criollo horses, and Solanet in turn will have lent his business a flourish of the epic. They left on April 23, 1925. They spent the first night in a monastery in an Irish community near Luján, not knowing at the time that the horses would return precisely to that town after they were dead, this second time to live through contretemps in their taxidermied versions. In Tschiffely's opinion, and in keeping with the complementary logic that underlies so many paternal gazes, Gato was mild-mannered, timid, keen, and tame, whereas Mancha was protective, extroverted, dominant, and alert. A two-year journey, an endless number of adventures and perils. They arrived in New York and Washington D.C. as heroes. Medals, conferences, photos, journalists, official receptions. The two horses and the Swiss-Englishman dressed up as a gaucho, all three with furnishings and trappings donated by Argentinean collectors. An epic of sentimental proportions that counteracted the speed of the automobile and the transformations of modernity. From that journey there remained, among other things, Tschiffely's tale with a preface by Cunningham Graham, the taxidermied horses in the Udaondo Museum, a portrait of the horses by Luis Cordiviola, a great business deal for Solanet and his heirs, a collection of little dolls of Mancha and Gato in miniature that an Englishwoman with teary eyes ordered from the company Julip Horses, a series of horrific monuments in three Argentinean cities, and a brand of Cordovan alfajores.

(After Aimé Tschiffely, *The Tale of Two Horses: A 10,000 Mile Journey as Told by the Horses* Equestrian Travel Classics, The Long Riders' Guild Press, September 2001.)

• • •

She places her hand on Gato's leg, palpates it as if she were one of those large animal vets she once saw on the television station *Canal Rural*. These horses definitely have all their bones, she concludes, that desperate man invented that story about the candelabras to get out of a bind, to change the subject. Was it also a lie that they were in Madison Square Garden? Still holding onto the horse's leg she transports herself, like an indigenous psychic, to the bar that was a few blocks from the stadium, her favorite refuge every time she had to be in New York City. Mara liked it because it seemed bizarrely embedded in those blocks that were otherwise set up as tourist-traps. As soon as the conference or the meeting or the summit or whatever was over, she would scurry over there and settle in for a long time at the bar, which for her functioned as a kaleidoscope: as the drinks began to take effect she would find more curiosities among the abundance of objects, pennants, good-luck charms, signed photographs, movie posters, and newspaper articles on display behind the bartender, if you could call that character a bartender. It was like sinking into an old-fashioned children's game. Every once in a while she'd talk to somebody, or rather, listen. A women once told her that her life was being destroyed by a tattoo, something like a mermaid that started in her pubic area and continued up to the base of her throat. For years she had felt accompanied and even protected by this figure, but now, when she had fallen in love for the first time in her life, she couldn't help but feel that her boyfriend was less with her than with the tattoo, the mermaid, especially in bed. Mara thought that actually the best sexual experiences arise from these kinds of displacements, but she didn't say anything. Perhaps that bar functioned for her as a kind of training platform, now that she thinks about it, her first exercises in the art of remaining silent in public. Her bar companion dug deep into a detailed account of her consultations with experts who had promised to leave her without a trace of the mermaid using a wide range of methods and at various prices. That's why she had traveled from her small town to New York City, because here she'd found a more reliable expert. She wasn't going to pinch pennies for something like that. While the items behind the bar continued to show her new facets, connections, nuances, Mara remembers having thought that the girl should simply admit that she likes group sex, but she didn't say that, either. She was wondering why people in the States tended to turn everything into a petty moral dilemma when the girl asked her to accompany her to the bathroom, she needed to show Mara the tattoo so she would be able to offer her verdict on the value of the mermaid. If she wasn't able to confront the truth with a stranger and far away from her hometown, she would never confront it, she insisted, and that sentence sounded to Mara like it was a line from a dubbed movie. The bathroom was tiny. The tattooed girl spent a long time trying to pull off a very tight T-shirt kind of thing, a garment that resisted her efforts, clinging to her body. When she finally managed, Mara had to agree that the mermaid, truth be told, was much more attractive than her bar companion, but she can't remember if this was the bit she avoided telling her.

TWO

THE FONDLY HELD BELIEF that one must consider the phases of the moon when deciding when to plant, not to mention doing so in coordination with a lunar eclipse, she reads, are mere superstitions. Mara is taking notes. The only thing she knows about gardening is that you shouldn't plant during months that have the letter *r*, though at this point she wonders if this one thing she knows might also belong in the category of superstitions. She doesn't care. It's a cold morning, she has two days off, and here is this yard she will convert into a garden-laboratory. She keeps reading her gardening manual. Just like with the rhetoric manual, the only other book she brought with her on this experiment year, her intention is to follow word for word the instructions of the Boutelous. That will allow her to see how the flowers described therein grow in other latitudes, in a different century, at other temperatures. Or how they don't grow, she couldn't care less about results. What interests her is to witness the process, the chimerical exercise, the slight distortion that will result from fanatically following a manual written in a different era, in the other hemisphere. She lingers on pages chosen at random: for a long time now her relationship with what she reads is marked by caprice. Never again that business of swallowing whole texts that would help her understand, the next day when she was shut away in her booth, the issues being talked about, the implicit understandings, and the proper nouns that occur with the most predictable frequency. She gets up to make more tea. The walls of the house and the high ceilings hold the cold, and for a moment she is tempted to press herself against one of them, emulating a kind of insect she doesn't know, one with sticky tentacles that stores the cold internally, as a protection against the torrid months, which will be here soon enough, she has just realized. She keeps leafing through the pages of the manual, the *Treatise on flowers: wherein is explained the methods of growing ornamental garden plants.* She particularly notes the names of some of the species mentioned by the two Boutelous, the book's coauthors: Mirror of Venus, Hoary Stock, Four O'Clock Flower, Dogtooth Violet, Red Hot Cat's Tail, Aztec Marigold, Chinese Aster, Cramp Bark, Naked Ladies. She is going to devote herself to these, not to roses or irises or all the others they also mention. What might those Boutelous have been to each other, she wonders? Brothers, father and son, cousins? And which one did the actual writing? Or did they divide up the chapters? She knows she could find out, even the answer to that last question, if she wanted, but no, better not. She prefers to imagine them sharing some undefined bond, elegant, dining formally every night, with no trace on their hands of having ever touched dirt or water or mud.

• • •

Recently, just a few days ago, she decided to start her botanical experiment sooner, right after her boss called her in for a meeting to give her news that supposedly would make her happy. Starting next week, she will be spending half the work day assisting a taxidermist they've finally hired to restore Mancha and Gato, like new. That's what she said: like new. Then, in her office warmed by two electric heaters, she enthusiastically launched into a detailed description of the efforts the director has been making for years to improve the condition of those horses and other pieces and the museum in general. At some point she started going into details about Mara's new responsibilities as an assistant and, in the final sluggish stretch, she descended into a mumbled monologue marked by something akin to pedagogical pride. Afterwards Luisa explained to her that the director of the museum had received a donation, or a grant, she didn't remember exactly, money, in any case, to restore the horses that had been so badly damaged in the flood a couple of decades ago, in the eighties if she remembered correctly, she was very young at the time. Mara knew that promotions were compulsively given at large corporations, but she never thought that would also be the case at a provincial museum in decline. In fact, that's why she chose a place like this, a place where nobody was obsessed with improving their position or their salary or their image or their quota or their level of English or their contacts or their skin or their education or their muscle tone or their networks or their car or their house or their speech or their efficiency or their manners or their memories or their nutrition or their words or their prosthesis or their posture. And now, suddenly, something was intervening that promised to improve not only her working conditions but also the condition of the embalmed horses in

her room, those horses inexorably in decline, which she had
somehow begun to grow fond of. Or something akin to fondness. She keeps staring at her future garden. She was always
absolutely clear that her experiment in detachment would not
be the practice of an ascetic in a tower or a fugitive in the for-
est: what interested her was to practice the art of remaining
silent while interacting with the world. But from the beginning she was also quite clear that those others would circulate
on parallel tracks, never interfering in her life, her everyday
existence, and it is precisely this, the implicit interruption, that
she now finds intolerable about this job as assistant, which has
just been dumped her. It took her months to decide what job
would best suit her experiment, months, until one day the job
of museum guard appeared on the horizon. And another few
months to get it, to fabricate dates, to clear up any suspicions.
She goes to get a glass of cold water, ice water, that freezing
cold liquid that goes directly into the middle of the forehead,
to clear things up. She should really give that garden a chance;
find out if for her, like for so many others, it offers some kind
of answer, inspiration, or solace, the little plants, which she has
no idea if they'll grow, appeasing her rage. But she doubts it.
She recalls her other manual, the one of rhetoric, and the passage that had been crucial when she started to enact her plan,
initiate her gesture that would go against the grain. This, her
fetishized passage, describes the impact an instant of silence and,
in turn, of stillness, can have in the middle of an enthusiastic
and fluent oration, one of those instants when the orator spaces
out, distracted by something much more interesting or revealing or urgent than what she was talking about, something she
will not mention when she takes up her speech but that will be

inevitably eloquent, triggering the broadest array of hypotheses. That instant—that gesture—is what Mara was seeking by coming here, and she figured that she needed one year to fine tune it. This business of having to be somebody's assistant, having to talk to him, deal with messages and give reports, was, at the very least, an interference. No: an interruption. No: an unforgiveable insult.

• • •

From the *Notebook*:

The ambiguous expression of Huysmans's character, Des Esseintes: a mixture of fatigue and ingenuity. Not the slightest trace of ambiguity, however, in his plan for total isolation. Reasons for his fatigue: the present day, new idolatries, new anxieties, murky conventions, stupidity, gossip, ignorance, provincialism, the city laid to waste. Leave Paris, leave Paris urgently. Leave and isolate himself. Conditions of his isolation: a modest house in Fontenay-aux-Roses, a couple of servants living upstairs, specially designed shoes for said servants so he doesn't even need to hear their footsteps, a very select collection of paintings and books. Obsession with Gordon Pym, admiration for Baudelaire, fascination with Petronius's absent plotline and Jan Luyken's gloomy fantasy. The shadows, darkness, a fondness for the Devil. Rereads, re-listens to, mentally reviews episodes in his life. Nothing to do in his fortress but spend the days lost in one of those works, his favorites. But cracks in the plan for perfect isolation begin to show. He attempts a trip: his phobia of traveling. He buys a plant collection: he tires of plants. The neuroses increase, multiply, sharpen. Everything goes wrong, the cracks deepen, the plan fails. Definitive interruption. Escape followed by perfect isolation fails. They say—Sylvia Molloy says—that Latin American writers of the nineteenth century admired Huysmans but couldn't rewrite him. In the twenty-first century someone, like a duelist, picks up the glove.

(After J. K. Huysmans, *Against the Grain*.)

• • •

Now she finally understands those women who sweep the sidewalks in front of their houses every Sunday; their efforts are no longer unfathomable. There's fury, anger, rage, furiously angry rage behind it. Mara moves her chair to sweep underneath, and over there also, between all the wheels on almost all the furniture in her museum room. As she sweeps she touches those pieces with her broom, raising dust, disobeying as she sweeps all the rules they explained to her the first day. She almost knocks over the bust of Carola Lorenzini with a movement of her elbow, as if the poor thing hadn't already suffered enough from her fatal fall. She tries to dust the wheels of the snowplow, the first one that went to the South Pole, and when she approaches those wheels wrapped in chains so they could move through not only the snow but also the unknown, she feels like climbing aboard, shifting into first gear, and driving out of this room, plowing everything out of her way: exhibits, staff, visitors, stray dogs, other exhibits, thin walls, cabinets, street vendors, shop windows, street signs, more exhibits, hired help, cultural tourists, security people, suppliers, researchers, more exhibits, restorers, taxidermists, management personnel, whole collections not on display, collections on display, presidential carriages, assistants, possible donors, junk, one-of-a-kind pieces, onward and onward, flattening all of it and everything else, onward, to the Soviet steppes such tractors know so well, onward to the island of Sakhalin and who knows where else. Someone pssts to her from the door. She stops and hears someone asking her what she is doing, in a tone of voice marked by that prosody of reprobation, which only guards who belong to the category "replacements" have the right to use, a category that does not underscore, in this universe, the implied precariousness of the terms of their employment but rather other connotative lines that are much more *à la page*, such as nomadism, diversity, transculturalism; also, as opposed to simple guards, who spend hours sitting on their only chair, replacements circulate from room to room, as well as alternate between the front door, the boss's office, the garden if the weather is good, the security post, even the director's study, and in so doing, their permanently nomadic state lends them power because of its implicit cosmopolitanism and their resulting privileged access to gossip. Replacements are the divas of the guards, and they know it, and from that position this particular one asks Mara what she is doing, why she is cleaning the room today when cleaning day was yesterday. Mara stands there staring at her as if instead of listening to a weekly work schedule, she were attending a keynote address on mathematics. The information reaches her as remote, incomprehensible. She releases one of her hands that was clutching the broom tightly. She looks at her palm, her fingers. Because of the pressure, she thinks, she must have cut off her circulation, and this has given them a strange, unrecognizable shape and color; her hand reminds her of a picture of a prehistoric species that she once saw in a scientific magazine.

. . .

From the *Notebook*:

Flight plans. No other kind. Two sentences are enough to complete the biography of Carola Lorenzini (future project: a book of microbiographies). No indication that she was ever interested in anything other than flying. But Carola L. was neither Amelia Earhart nor Beryl Markham but rather a girl in San Vicente, Argentina, in the nineteen-thirties—no famous publicist, no celebrated mentor to ease her way. Every day she had to go to her job in an office at the telephone company, every day. Morning after morning, like Kafka, Huysmans, Borges, Martínez Estrada, Cavafy. Office hours, office interruptions, and the one benefit: to pay for her pilot training course. She received her license, broke records, established flight paths, organized a mission to unite fourteen provinces, famously perfected the inverted loop. She was the only one who could perform that highly dangerous aerobatic maneuver besides her teacher, Santiago Germanó, who lifted hats and even scarves when he scrapped along the ground with his airplane in reverse. Carola L. became a local celebrity. She would land in an open field and people would run to see her, attribute superpowers to her, bless her, ask her to cure various illnesses, believe in her, think she performed miracles. In order to avoid accidents, Carola L. always tried to land at some distance from these fans who were waiting for her, then she'd get on a horse and ride to them: precautionary strategies that could be read as a mise-en-scène, or that had the same effect. She did all of that while still needing to work at the telephone company. One of Carola L.'s mornings in the office. Efficient, affable, lighthearted: this was how she behaved at work, nothing to indicate a misunderstood or striving diva. Nevertheless, with time and among female aviators who came to see her as an icon, today brought together in OR-FEA (*Organización Femenina de Aeronavegantes*, Organization of Female Pilots), there is an hypothesis that behind those good manners, behind that desk in the office, she accumulated rage, a lot of rage. Rage against the head of the telephone company, against the leaders of the Air Force. Rage against prohibitions and exclusions, against suspensions and a lack of systemic support: the interrupters and the great versatility of their efforts to stand in the way. According to the same hypothesis, so much rage that Carola L. wrongly calculated the inverted loop at that show where she was invited at the last moment and after some arm twisting. Fury rather than incompetence as the cause of the fatal accident, according to the women of ORFEA.

(After Laura Isola, "*La paloma gaucha*," *Radar* magazine, Buenos Aires, April 20, 2003.)

• • •

She finds an insect she has never seen before. Might this be what has resulted from those seeds she planted? An insect with improbable legs, as if drawn in zigzags? She looks at the rows in search of something, a tiny sign, any kind of confirmation that she did, indeed, plant the first seeds of her experimental garden months ago, but nothing. Only a never-before-seen insect. Might this be what they call the margin of unpredictability? She kills it immediately. She doesn't care if it was a derivative of her experiment: she is not Dr. Frankenstein, she can easily destroy the undesired results. She looks at the yard to see where her new flower, La Extraña, also called the Queen Margaret Astor, will do best. According to the Boutelous, it can reach a height of two meters and will have "a thick, fuzzy stalk with many side branches and leaves alternate, ovate, and smooth, almost as long as they are wide, pointed, with unevenly toothed edges, and held by thick, winged petioles." She plants the seeds in rows: the description suggests that the time will come when a section of her garden will be full of Las Extrañas that will be taller than her, a veritable vegetal fortress. Though she cannot yet be certain, the latest news does not preclude the possibility that she will have to abandon this garden in its infancy long before she planned to. Allow weeds and insects to grow, truncate her experiment in detachment. Just the thought of it outrages her, though this does nothing to shake her out of the confusion that was the source of her initial fury. She first sits then lies down on the ground. She reads again: "The disk florets are tubular, hermaphroditic and yellow, and ringed by ray florets, forming the ligules, which are feminine; the receptacle is naked, and the seeds are topped with downy pappus." At moments this manual of the Boutelous, she thinks, reads like an undercover Kama Sutra.

· · ·

She opens the door and is surprised to see Ringo; someone else, an errand boy of sorts, delivered the last few orders. For some reason she can't figure out, he launches into an account of how busy he's been, making plans for new deliveries to nearby towns to the west. Maybe he decided to adopt this grandiose air in order to tolerate the fact that he ended up accepting the conditions imposed by his father. Now, in fact, after delivering her order, he's going back there, Ringo adds. Maybe she wants to come with him, it's her day off, if he remembers correctly. Mara, to her own surprise, immediately agrees: she needs to get some air, rise to the occasion, overcome this hurdle. The path of tranquility has never been her specialty, but, as some say, it can provide counsel. From the passenger seat of a four-wheel-drive vehicle with the view of an airplane cockpit she is surprised to realize how quickly one can get out of town. She says this and not much else. Ringo doesn't, either. Both stare absentmindedly at the road, and Mara thinks that she would give anything to have a friend to not talk to. But, after the first gas station, Ringo returns to the expansive version of himself. He wants her to know that in the last few months he has found a way to solve his problem with his parents. The one about his studies. Something tells him that this time he can trust her, her judgment. Mara utters an onomatopoeia that she's not sure registers with him. Very simple: he stopped ignoring one of his mother's new friends, another member of the counter-ur-banization, or re-ruralization, sect that left good jobs in trans-national companies to come to this place and grow vegetables. What they didn't take into account was how bored they'd be. They didn't take it into account and they don't admit to it; but he sees them, he sees them dying of boredom. He's seen it in his parents all these years, and he keeps seeing it in those new friends who are following the same trend: the fake naïveté when they try to learn a trade, the overvaluing of the trades, the overlapping bodywork seminars given by people for whom they feel actual disdain, disdain above all, deep disdain that deep down they have for everything around them, the poorly disguised paternalism, the dead time when they realize that even though they moved and changed their occupation, they're getting old anyway. For a second Mara is tempted to ask him what he wants to study, what is it that his father is so dead set against, but she fears that a single question would initiate a dialogue protocol when she can barely deal with the monologues. It's been a while now since he started to notice, Ringo continues, that one of these new friends of his parents, a psychoanalyst who says she got tired of treating neurotics and now wants to give classes in social psychology or something of the sort, chose him as an antidote to her boredom. She recommended books, discussed movies with him, she even tried to mediate when the conflict with his parents started to intensify. As far as he was concerned this woman was just another nuisance, until a light bulb went on in his head. Okay, he thought, he would be her sex toy, but she would be the card up his sleeve. Now the time has come for him to start dropping hints that will make his parents suspect that something might be going on between him and the psychoanalyst, as, in fact, there is. It's very important that they suspect something before anything else. If he shoves it in their face, the effect will be lost. A hint dropped here, a bit of evidence there, he has to advance and retreat, advance and retreat, give the subject all the time it needs. If he can manage that, the rest will be simple; his parents, who deep down haven't changed one bit, will be horrified at the prospect of looking bad in front of their friends, especially the whole group of friends who share all the new arrivals and who took them so much effort to calibrate, and they'll have no choice but to give in to his blackmail and allow him to leave. But since that alone won't guarantee that it remains a secret, Ringo will raise the stakes: he'll be able to study what he wants to study and won't have to work. He's convinced that he's in an optimum negotiating position. Mara interrupts him to say that she's getting off there, thank you very much, she always dreamed of spending a night in a hotel in this small town where they have just arrived.

• • •

They bring her the remote control along with the croissants and coffee. Mara assumes she should take it as a gesture of good will and that's the only reason she changes the channel. The truth is it's all the same to her if she eats breakfast with that dubbed movie or a soccer game or an account of the latest catastrophe, exactly the same. Rather than a television at breakfast she expected a town newspaper full of salacious headlines and poorly written ledes. At another time she would have asked for a newspaper, or she would have been out buying one at the corner. At another time she would have asked for a different room. Asking for a different room had become a habit. Million-dollar negotiations, treaties that had been discussed for months and even years, strategic alliances, revolutionary experiments, and opportune career maneuvers could fail if the interpreters did not have all their faculties working when they started to interpret. Sentences like that one were often brandished at three in the morning in front of desk clerks who were as polite as they were impenetrable. By the time she got what she wanted it was five, and she had two hours to sleep, at the most. She hears laughter behind her. Only then does she realize that she is not alone in the dining room. Apparently the regular patron found that something said on TV was funny. He says something to her, but she can't make it out. She turns around and smiles, as if she agrees.

• • •

The bus drops her off at the central bus station around five. Before getting on another one that will take her back to the small town where she lives, she decides to wander around there a little, in the vicinity of the museum, in the area she usually systematically avoids. She walks through what they call the park, along the banks of what they call the river. Two open-air garbage dumps. She steps around small plastic and glass bottles, wine cartons, bags containing unidentifiable scraps, and other bad aftertastes of the weekend. At least there's nobody around, she manages to think at the very same moment she sees three people implacably approaching her. Her new boss—the taxidermist—is in the middle, wearing a hat that doesn't even remotely address the diffident sun these days. He walks with fake self-confidence. The day the director introduced them he seemed a little less pompous. Mara regrets taking this detour: now she's the one putting her protocol of muteness and quietude in danger. The first inklings of Stockholm Syndrome. She manages to increase her pace, to simulate an athletic rhythm that nothing or nobody should interrupt, but the path along the river is narrower than she thought, and she is intercepted. The taxidermist is euphoric under his hat. He introduces her to his companions as the person who has the honor of looking after Mancha and Gato. He introduces the man on his right as the president of an association whose name means nothing to Mara, though she immediately deduces that it's the one that has made the donation that Luisa told her about. The woman on his left must be his wife, also according to Luisa, but he doesn't introduce her, perhaps so as not to disturb her: she seems to be thousands of kilometers away from there. Mara would prefer her to be the one speaking, at least so she could find out if it is true that she's a foreigner, and above all so she could guess where she's from. One of her favorite hobbies in her former life consisted of guessing the native language behind the Spanish she was listening to. She got so she could guess not only the most obvious source languages but also Lithuanian, Zulu, Ilocano, and a dialect that is still spoken on a remote Polynesian island. But the woman is nowhere near uttering a word: she is looking toward the river, though her eyes aren't focused on anything in particular. She must be about her age, Mara figures, late thirties, but she still has childlike features. Something even seems to indicate that she will be like this till the end, that with the passage of time she will become a wrinkled little girl, an oxymoron in a face. A wax face, Mara thinks, exactly like a wax doll. The taxidermist is telling her that this man is a prominent lawyer and also one of the most active members of such-and-such association. Then he reminds her of the day and the hour he expects her in his cabinet, the same way he reminded her a few days ago in front of the museum director, and the same way he must have spoken in the meeting with her boss. It's fundamental that from the beginning she be clear about what her work schedule will be. Mara cracks a smile as she reviews the definition of one of the ten types of silence defined in her manual of rhetoric, the first: "Silence is prudent when we know how to not speak in an opportune way, according to the moment and the place in which we find ourselves in the company of others, and according to the consideration we must show to persons with whom we are forced to deal and live." She can't wait to start, says her future boss, and looks at the lawyer, his jaw tense. Mara mumbles some excuse and continues on her way.

• • •

From the *Notebook*:

A. F. Tschiffely chooses an odd form of autobiography: a series of portraits of characters he knew throughout his life. Despite their important differences, they are all people who share the furtive impulse, who reject a useful life: advocates for a lack of productivity or the dregs of productivity that are still circulating within the most settled bastions of the era of progress. In this version of Tschiffely, few references to his equestrian adventures. In contrast to the gaucho patina of his Latin American costume. Tschiffely as a collector of characters, his only true passion other than boxing. A few in this prolific series: Jim the Anthropoid, the geologist he met at a bar in some Pacific port, to whom he gave that nickname to distinguish him from his inseparable companion, Jim the Monkey, with whom he came to the bar every afternoon to drink rum, a lot of rum, both the same amount, until inevitably they began to argue and then Jim the Monkey would go into fits of rage, grab his head, and begin to scream "like one of Dante's condemned souls." His inseparable companion, in the meantime, would sit silently on his stool, his legs crossed, staring at the continuous and slight movements of his own right foot. That image, says Tschiffely when he writes his autobiography more than twenty years later, "still haunts me, obsesses me." Another: the sinologist from New York who spent a few days in Lima, a change from his repeated trips to China, and dragged Tschiffely to the most out-of-the-way places in Lima's Chinatown, where he spent his time bartering in Chinese with experienced antiques dealers, and afterwards, when he was tired of winning or losing, he took him to taste Chinese delicacies and later to the opium dens where tourists never go. And where, he insisted, one could feel much closer to China. Another: Sophocles, a fellow boarder in London, an elusive and chameleonic friend who insisted on converting him to the spiritual teachings of Raymond Duncan, brother of Isadora, an experience Tschiffely finally agreed to, which obliged him to go to the Doré Galleries on Bond Street, where he tolerated the exclamations and exhortations of the New Prophet by imagining the moment he would return to the Boxing Academy, where, he was certain, the true masters could be found. And another one, even at the risk of infusing these notes with the collector's impulse: the "lonely drinker," who arrived every two or three months at the London boarding house where Tshiffely lived in order to spend a whole week drinking, shut away in his room. He always brought his own sheets and duvet, tins of caviar and lobster, crackers and butter; and in advance he ordered boxes of whisky, brandy, champagne, and Vichy water, which always arrived at the boarding house punctually, a couple of hours after his own arrival. He was well-mannered and wore good clothes: the only things, after years, that they were able to know about him.

(After A. F. Tschiffely, *Bohemia Junction*, London: Hodder & Stoughton, 1950.)

• • •

She has never been in this part of the museum, which means she has to wander around more than she would like to find what the taxidermist calls his cabinet. It looks more like the chamber where they put the crazy relative to do his occupational therapy, Mara thinks when she finally finds the door. He's not there and neither is anybody else. She decides to sit down and wait for him. After all, her lumbar contact doesn't discriminate among chairs. Maybe if she manages to remain centered, quiet, and almost motionless, even when working as an assistant, her plan will end up stronger. She must concentrate on pushing away the bad omens. She sits down. Her eyes are adjusting to the dark. Everything is more or less in a mess except for a heavy wood table in the middle of the room on which Mara can make out a number of tools, jars, a couple of receptacles, papers, and a file folder. Right in front of her is a wood platform, a kind of dais, as if someone were building a stage set. She hears persistent banging. She doesn't think she needs to respond. It continues, but she doesn't move. It doesn't seem to be coming from the door. She wonders if there might be rats in this place. Suddenly the door opens and the light that enters the room makes her squint. The taxidermist seems less aware of her presence than of the things he is carrying and doesn't know where on the table to leave them. He exhibits the kind of physical hesitation that often functions as an evasive way of asking for help, but she doesn't move. Then, while looking for something on his tool table, he repeats everything that has already been said about the timetable and their work schedule. He stresses the importance of meeting those deadlines, the overriding need to finish in time for the exhibition. He handed in his preliminary reports on time, but the museum bureaucracy has forced them to start a month later than planned. They will have to make up that time, take it from somewhere or other. He insists on the importance of the exhibition in December. He says a few more sentences about this, addressing her formally as *usted*, and then lists basic tools that he needs to always have on hand. He's certain none is missing, but in any case he needs Mara to check their condition and sort them out. He tells her to get some paper and jot down some notes, that's how she'll learn. As he dictates, there passes through Mara's head, crowded together or superimposed, the infinite number of times that her job consisted of studying without the time or curiosity or pleasure that are the basic requirements in other professions. The pedagogical method this man has now mentioned confirms the curse underlying this change, this interruption her boss calls a promotion. He supposes that by the end of this week, very soon, they will have brought him the horses, she hears him say; it's crucial that by then they have everything they need in the workshop. He has already prepared at home the formula he'll use to dampen the hides. The sentence shakes her out of her irritation. It becomes something else, a kind of alarm, a sign. It takes her a while to register exactly what it means, something in her system delays the information from reaching her. That has never happened to her before, ever. She would go so far as to invent sentences, misunderstand what she had to translate, translate a metaphor literally, get stuck in the most foreseeable blind alleys that stalk an interpreter, but she never had problems understanding what she was hearing. She would often even guess the next sentence in a speech or the response to a particular line of dialogue, and then she'd get ahead and save time. Suddenly, she hears the banging again. The taxidermist looks up, his face glowing. Mara sees that there is a small window she had not previously noticed, and a bird is furiously pecking at the glass and then retreating, recovering its strength, then throwing itself back into pecking with the same or more frenzy. A suicidal bird, that's the only explanation. The taxidermist asks if she sees it. When Mara mutters yes, he tells her that she is a lucky woman. Then he turns his back on her, as if putting an end to the conversation and the work session. Mara looks at her watch. According to the work schedule, there's still half an hour to go. It doesn't matter; she grabs her things and leaves.

• • •

She uses a napkin as a bookmark and closes the manual of the Boutelous—brothers, father and son, cousins? To follow word-for-word the instructions in a manual from a different place and remote era seems a lot like a literal translation, now that she thinks about it, and it's possible that the outcome of her garden will end up being the same sort of gibberish, but she couldn't care less. Thanks to this method she will establish a relationship with the flowers that will be utterly devoid of the customary connotations of a garden: ladies at leisure, eccentric gentlemen, magazines with shiny covers. But first she has to keep pulling the weeds. She brings a pitcher of cold water for her and Ringo, who's helping her. That morning, when he came with her order and she asked him if maybe he knew someone who did that kind of work, he offered to help. Not the next day and not later, at that very moment. He made a phone call and invented a problem with his truck that would prevent him from continuing with his deliveries, and his father believed him or pretended to. The yard work is exhausting, but that doesn't dissuade Ringo from continuing to recount to her in detail how he has advanced his strategy. Mara thinks that it's much better than watching a telenovela. She also thinks that she doesn't know if it's right to pull out all the weeds, some of them are quite attractive. She'd never looked at them up close before. One thing is the infuriatingly straight lines of a well-kempt lawn, another quite different is these weeds with patterned leaves and yellow, blue, and purple flowers. Still, she keeps pulling them out, and she finds something addictive about this repetitive act. When Ringo tells her that he's going to need to leave she realizes that it's getting dark. They sit there looking at the future garden, their backs against the cold wall that surrounds the yard. Ringo removes a bottle from his backpack and takes a few quick sips, like a mountain climber. She opens the manual again, this time to the chapter on Tenweeks Stock. "The stems of Tenweeks Stock grow to two feet, they are thick, branching, and with oblanceolate, hairy leaves that are sometimes alternate and sometimes opposite, and are often whorled. The flowers bloom in dense clusters, or racemes, which are fragrant and composed of four long-clawed petals. The seedpods are long, round, pointed, and scored, each containing numerous round, flat, and pubescent seeds." She would not tolerate this kind of baroque gloating in any other text, but here, in the Boutelous, it works particularly well: without being able to explain precisely why, something about this prose indicates to her that she should understand the descriptions as forecasts, so she reads the Boutelous as if they were tarot card readers whose every adjective predicts that she will have a lush, amnesic garden.

● ● ●

She should wait for him today in the museum workshops, outside the door, the taxidermist specified. He wants to speak directly to those two maintenance men who are supposed to move the horses to his cabinet, he doesn't understand why there are still delays. According to the director, the internal paperwork is complete, and the instructions are clearly spelled out, even she doesn't understand. This is not the first job he's done for the museum, he knows how to get things done around here, he says as he arrives, then walks away with a resolute step. Mara follows at a certain distance. At a particular moment, in fact, she loses sight of him. When she finds him again, he is sitting on one of the forsaken wooden benches in front of the door to the workshops. He motions with his head to indicate that she should sit down, too. They will wait until the workers arrive, they left for lunch, according to what he's been told. They won't move all afternoon, if necessary. Never, not in any of the many times Mara has come into this area to change her uniform without anybody seeing has she paid any attention to the garden she now has in front of her. She decides to recall at least ten names of species she can see, a trick that's not easy to pull off. She's on the third, she thinks, when the taxidermist gets up from the bench and starts pacing back and forth. With long strides, with bombastic gestures. He leaps from the workers taking a lunch break to the deterioration of the country. His voice is too loud, as if for a large audience. Mara manages to recall one further plant species, and then another. She decides to check that very night if they are described by the Boutelous. The taxidermist wants to know if Mara realizes to what extent this delay negatively effects not only the horses and his own work but the lives of each and every person in this country who wants to do things well. He should have left when he had the chance, if she only knew the offers he received from abroad, but no, always letting himself be carried along with that hope, that illusion, that sense of responsibility to make sure that the work of the few before him wouldn't vanish into thin air. His own grandfather—this is something she needs to know—was one of this country's pioneers, someone who never hesitated to risk everything for that ideal, one of those pioneers who penetrated into the deepest and most challenging regions of Patagonia. Right after he reached legal age, he enlisted in Ramón Lista's expedition. Those were truly brave young men, he insists, his stride now more relaxed. That's when his grandfather met Polidoro Segers, the expedition's doctor and the main reason why he as well as his father have devoted their lives to taxidermy. Better said, why they established the foundations of the profession of taxidermy here in Argentina. His grandfather helped Segers and also worshipped him, this in spite of the fact that the man was preceded by a story that didn't show him in the best light, but that's irrelevant now. He doesn't admire him at all, he simply knows how to proudly carry on the family profession. Mara considers this the perfect last sentence of his soliloquy, and in some way so does he, because he remains quiet for a few minutes, though only to change the subject and gather momentum. She should know, he says, that not only those workers who must be eating an entire deer judging from how long they're taking, not only those specific workers who will hear a piece of his mind when they deign to return, but each and every worker and employee who doesn't do his job, who is always trying to take advantage, is betraying all those people, everybody like his grandfather who believed that this could one day be a serious country. She needs to know this, he repeats, now without moving, on the verge of delivering a reprimand. Then he sits back down. So calm, so learned, he says. Never, not before or after that expedition, had he ever met anybody like Segers, his grandfather would repeat, and he followed him everywhere. He followed him everywhere, working as his assistant without anybody asking him to. She will soon see, by the way, what this job as assistant they've given her can teach her, or rather, offer her, allow her to see. Mara finally gives up, at least for the day, the game of naming plant species so that her mind can summarize, with precision, the eighth on the list of ten kinds of silence as defined in her manual of rhetoric: "A silence of contempt is one that does not deign to respond to those who speak to us or who expect us to give our opinion on a particular subject, and looks with as much coldness as pride at everything that comes from them." At Segers's side his grandfather saw a corpse for the first time, an incident that always remains in a child's memory. She surely remembers the first corpse she saw. In this case, it was a question of mortal remains. His grandfather described the scene to him only once, but he never forgot it. It could almost be said that the first corpse he himself saw was the same one, his grandfather's, that is, the one his grandfather saw, which was of a small Indian, a youth who had fought to the bitter end when his group confronted Lista's forces. To Segers, his grandfather told him, that death seemed like an act of the utmost cruelty, totally unnecessary, and so, when the men of the expedition went to sleep, Segers told him that the two of them were going to get up early the next day, much earlier than everybody else, and before setting out he was going to bury that boy with his own hands, he wasn't going to leave him to be eaten by scavengers. That whole night neither of them could sleep, and not only due to remorse but also because of the howls of a dog, the Indian's dog, a howl like the flaming of souls, something not of this world. For the rest of his life, he would hear that howl in his worst nightmares, his grandfather said. Identical, exact. They thought it would never stop, then suddenly, in the middle of the night, they ceased to hear it. Segers was worried: he assumed Lista's men had killed the dog as well, which meant that they'd gotten up before him, which in turn meant that there was no way they would be able to bury the bullet-ridden youth. He got up in the dark in an effort to try anyway, along with his grandfather, and that was when he saw the boy's corpse for the first time, or rather what was left of it. The dog, who wasn't dead as they had assumed, greeted them with a fierce glare. They say that he was eating every part of his owner that he possibly could, as if not wanting to leave even his dead body in the hands of those savages. Or maybe he was just hungry, says the taxidermist, and laughs to himself.

• • •

From the *Notebook*:
In order to confer greatness on the nation, the Institución Mitre planned a "Biographical Dictionary" and in 1932 called a

competition to pick its author. Out of all the candidates, they chose Udaondo, who wrote less of a dictionary and more of a "Who's Who" in the style of what had been published in England for more than fifty years. An institutionalized entre nous. A few years previously, Udaondo had written a book that catalogued the trees of Argentina, now he'd do the same with the characters. Among the 3,200 names is Polidoro Segers, who is portrayed in overblown prose. *Seggers*, with double *g*. A distraction? An added emphasis for a last name that seemed somehow lacking? According to this Who's Who, Dr. Polidoro was born in Belgium to a family of noblemen and heroes, arrived in Buenos Aires as a very young man, studied medicine, traveled to Patagonia with Lista's expedition as a surgeon, spent a long stretch of time in Tierra del Fuego, discovered the disease that caused a plague among the Ona Indians, found a way to cure it, returned to Paris, worked shoulder to shoulder with the famous Dr. Doyen, became a seminarian in Rome after his wife died, returned to Buenos Aires, completed his ecclesiastical studies there, and founded the laboratory of the History of Pathology. But it doesn't mention that he was a pianist, that he arrived in Buenos Aires for the first time as a member of a classical quartet based in Paris, and that he chose to remain behind when they finished their tour and the others returned. He was already a concert pianist, not an amateur, but he stayed. Nor does this dictionary say anything about his experiments with the embalming of dead bodies. The inevitable association Dr. Polidoro/Dr. Polidori: might there be implicit shame in some names? The only interesting part of a biography are those black holes—or whiteouts: the color scheme doesn't weaken the metaphor—but that is precisely the material that any Who's

Who dismisses. As ceremoniously as in the entries that follow, Udaondo asserts in the "Notice" at the beginning of the book that it took him five years to write it, that he consulted the widest possible range of archives and witnesses, and that he devoted the time "we had free from other occupations." First person plural as a gesture of erasure, false modesty, a convention of the era, undoubtedly. But just before closing the book, before apathetically scanning a few entries, right then and there, like a flash, a suspicion, a ghost, some kind of associative mechanism leads me to Leiva. Rosendo Leiva, the scribe who was responsible for the daily operations of the museum, the reports, the gazettes, the accounts, the daily minutiae. The painstaking penmanship of his letters, the patience of a detective that he exhibited in that accumulation of data. I go back and leaf through this tome and that's what appears before me, what I see, traces of Leiva. Not the least sign of Udaondo's performative eloquence. The first person plural is also a wink, an expression of gratitude to his faithful scribe, that's how I read it, independent of dates and other kinds of assertions.

(After Enrique Udaondo, *Diccionario Biográfico Argentino*, Buenos Aires: Coni, 1938.)

• • •

Mara takes her time reading the options on the menu. What she likes about this restaurant is that it doesn't try to disguise the junk food or, even less, emphasize it in order to make the popular seem eccentric, an overused act of chicanery she knew from her previous travels. Luisa insists that she tell her all about her new job as assistant. Not much more than she's already told her, she mumbles, a sentence Mara always knew how to wield when she was perfectly aware of having said nothing, or almost nothing, about whatever it was. She's just waiting for it to end, for these months to go by quickly, she adds. She sees the door to the restaurant open: again, the taxidermist, his wife, and the lawyer. Again, her boss wearing a hat, this time some kind of panama. He greets her with a smile and approaches her table. He wants to tell her that the day before, when she had to go to her room and those workers still hadn't appeared, he had a brilliant idea: he went down to the river, found a couple of bums who are always hanging around there, and arranged for them to move the horses to his cabinet in exchange for a couple of bottles of cheap wine. He snaps his fingers and says that in a split second, in the blink of an eye, he'd arranged everything. He seems to doubly enjoy this rudimentary process, as if in this way he is more blatantly exposing the ruinous state from which he is rescuing those pieces and restoring them to perfection. He is still addressing her formally as usted, but for some reason that Mara can't quite put her finger on, the taxidermist wants to suggest in front of his wife or the lawyer a camaraderie they don't actually share. This results in the total shut-down of her stomach, so she orders the special without even bothering to find out what it is. Luisa says that up close he's a lot nicer than she thought, though the same does not apply to his wife. Recently she saw her at the hardware store buying plaster and other materials, and she paid special attention to her. She's not exaggerating when she says that it's the first time in years that she's seen her do anything on her own in town. Either she's not seen at all for months on end, or she's with him, but only to run errands like that, she has never run into her at the supermarket or getting a manicure or anywhere else. She seems like a captive. But not a suffering captive, rather a pedantic one, an imperious captive. If it weren't for Mara, she would have almost forgotten about her and the taxidermist. He was away for years, more than ten for sure, then one day he returned with this woman. He left on bad terms with his family: with his father because they do the same work, and with his son because he doesn't do anything, that's all she remembers.

• • •

Now, finally, yes, finally, he mutters as he paces around the table. He rearranges, searches, classifies, takes notes, all while constantly humming. Mara and the two horses watch him, all three immobile. It's so good she can work on weekends, so good, he says, so they can spend these two days preparing the room. To think that in less that forty-eight hours he will be starting his real job, finally. His work, he corrects himself. Now, finally, yes. She is a lucky one, he doesn't know if she's realized that yet. Apprentices from all over the world line up to watch him work, yes, they line up. He's already received messages from several applicants who heard that he'll be working on the famous Mancha and Gato. But he doesn't want one of those pretend assistants, whiners who are just waiting for when they can claim some of the credit, that's why he asked for a museum guard. And her boss especially recommended her, congratulations, he tells her. Thanks to his own wisdom about the human animal, she has reaped the rewards, she has made an inconceivable leap. What they call a stroke of luck, the kind that happens only very rarely. He hopes he doesn't have to explain that everything related to this job must remain strictly between them. She'll see, she'll see with her own eyes the transformation those horses will undergo, and one day she'll be able to tell her grandchildren that it was due to her, in part. To think that they were poor beasts of burden, handled by Indians, gauchos, everybody, and they are now broadening their range, evolving. Now people pay to see their dexterity, he asserts, and he makes a gesture that reminds Mara of a concierge at an expensive hotel. He shows her three mounds of various sizes and asks her to check the aniline dyes. One by one, and she should write down the date of fabrication and expiration. Then he very carefully opens a can with a faded label and takes out something wrapped in layers of paper, something Mara can't quite see. With those horses, we really see that not all is lost, there are still ways of avoiding the decay that surrounds us, he continues. And he is more than proud to contribute to this cause: in this taxidermy, in fact, he will be working in a direct line from Tschiffely. No, not really that wayward gringo, but rather Don Emilio Solanet. Thanks to him the Criollo race stopped roaming wild or working in the fields, being ruined by lazy peasants. When she's finished with those pliers she should start counting the tacks, he adds, without lifting his eyes from what he took out of that can, a piece he seems to be working on. Mara goes over to the pile of tacks and embarks on the task of organizing them. From this angle, she verifies, the horses look bigger and more exhausted. The idea of returning to her post and leaving them there, at the mercy of the taxidermist, gives her an indecipherably uncomfortable feeling, or something worse than uncomfortable, though she couldn't say what that is. From where she sits she sees that the taxidermist is working on a bird; probably another project, one of those small orders one usually takes to work on during the down time that often occurs, which is often even required, while working on a bigger job. The taxidermist is talking about how he learned everything he knows through observation. His father did and he watched. Then come a string of afternoons spent in a ramshackle old shed his mother had to drag them out of to get them to come eat. Mara wonders if the inevitable correlative of this practice might be verbosity, the sound of one's own voice acting as affirmation that one is alive even while working all day with dead bodies. In her previous mental construct, taxidermists were solitary, taciturn, silent people. Of course she had never come across one in the flesh, not even on one of those temp jobs she used to do while she was studying. A cell phone rings, the taxidermist goes outside to the museum patio. The semidarkness returns along with the silence. Mara sighs with relief and looks up at the high window, the only one through which a little light enters. It seems odd to her that the suicidal bird hasn't appeared even once that afternoon.

· · ·

From the *Notebook*:

Five toes, like all of us: the first horses of the Americas had five toes. They called them Phenacodus, and they lived in North America millions of years ago. Millions of years, more than forty million. So it's a common mistake to think that the first horses came from Europe. So says Carlos Rusconi, a paleontologist because at an early age he read Florentino Ameghino, the man who defended the hypothesis that the most ancient human in the world was born on Argentine soil. Rusconi wanted to be an artist, they didn't let him. As a paleontologist and geographer, he said that the Criollo horse could be a descendent of the North American Phenacodus. He also said that, just as there were horses in North America more than forty million years ago who later spread to the south, there were also camels, but they didn't spread. Why the one and not the other? If they had both spread, fixation on the patriotic equine would have dissipated, there would have been a bifurcation, an alternation, a cohabitation of quadrupeds capable of carrying us at high speeds as well as performing other functions, among them the symbolic one, and this perhaps would have led to a more diverse, more cosmopolitan cultural configuration. The nation would have been different if the camel had also spread. But it didn't, only the horse did, according to Rusconi, who wanted to be an artist and they didn't let him. Why did one spread and the other didn't? Instead of those equines with long faces, we would be surrounded by camelids, those animals with a serpentine mouth, two humps, a perfect anus. Bruce Chatwin, appreciated for having *the* eye—that talent to appreciate art that made him famous among London gallery owners and collectors—said that he had never seen anything more perfect than the anus of a camel.

(After Carlos Rusconi, *Animales extinguidos de Mendoza y de la Argentina*, Mendoza: publisher unknown, 1967.)

• • •

She measures six fingers and makes a mark in the dirt, another six and another mark, and so on. What Mara finds interesting about her garden experiments is that they allow her to do one thing while she thinks about other things. Now she plants rows of Four O'Clocks, whose flowers open only after the sun sets, according to the Boutelous. She will be able to enjoy peaceful insomnia: she'll come out to the yard and there will be flowers, open for the sole purpose of calming her spirit, a thought that brings anticipated relief. Everything indicates that the season of insomnia that began with the interruption of her new job won't end either soon or easily. It will not end, in fact, until she thinks of something, until she finds a way to respond, react, attack, defend, some way to interrupt this interruption, some variation on this gesture of hers that goes against the grain. Then she makes a small hole in each of the spots marked in the dirt and plants fistfuls of seeds. She bought them at the town nursery according to the Latin name. Or what she thinks is the Latin name of the Boutelous' flowers, which in turn she needs to translate into the Spanish of a rural town. She didn't ask the salesperson anything at all: she doesn't want anything to come between her and the Boutelouian instructions. According to them, in addition to the six fingers between plants, one must also keep in mind "timely waterings, weeding, and the light labor of almocafre." Mara hasn't the slightest idea what "almocafre" is, and she doesn't want to find out. She prefers to stick with the "light labor," which sounds quite good to her. "In northern climes, where these plants die due to the severity of the cold, they are stored in sand in a sheltered spot during the winter." The approach of spring puts her senses as well as her phobias on high alert: she would give anything to live in a country where cold prevails, as well as long nights and clothes that are barely distinguishable from blankets, hats an absolute necessity, quick steps, an accidental encounter on the street addressed with a mere nod of the head. Instead, she's chosen this path that leads to the tropics. How sad is our Russia, as Honoria says. Mara knows where that quote comes from, but she prefers to ascribe it to this woman who—she hasn't yet figured out why—made such a good impression on her.

• • •

From the *Notebook*:

Two volumes and almost seven hundred pages: nobody, it seems, was as devoted to writing about their own garden as Alphonse Karr. Writing about it and cultivating it, wherever and however. On the French Riviera, where he moved in 1855, and before that in Paris, in his tiny apartment in Montmartre, where he and his monkey could barely fit, but where there was enough room for a garden with plants and a grotto and a fountain. And in his house on rue de La Tour-d'Auvergne, where he lived with a mulatto servant dressed á la oriental. And in a seventh floor apartment on rue Vivienne, where he created a garden on the balcony, one of those spaces stolen from the cement, from the association, from the surveys and the regulations. Clandestine gardens. The connection between those places stolen from the commons and the crime pages of the newspaper: the little girl who disappeared in her own building and the concierge who kept swearing till the last moment that it was her pet that she had buried on her terrace on the top floor (Milan, 2009); the thieves convinced that money was hidden under the squares of sod and who forced the retired man to lift them up one by one until he had a heart attack (Buenos Aires, 2007); the attendant at the gas station with a far-away look in his eyes who managed to bury in his green and lush parcel up to twenty-three pinkies of the teenage boys he had murdered over a period of fifteen years (Minneapolis, 1997). It's true what Karr stated implicitly in his seven hundred pages: a great many things happen in gardens. His *Voyage autor de mon jardin* was written in parallel with the journey of a friend of his around the world, expending energy and obliged to take notes, while he, on the other hand, could imagine. "Travelers claim they have seen Cyclopes; those who travel around their room, on the other hand, describe spiders as Cyclopes": one of Karr's good sentences. Then he wrote others, an endless number, and became a coiner of aphoristic phrases and a propagandist, which is sometimes the same thing. The deep malaise one of those sentences provoked in José Martí in 1871, when he was a law student in exile in Madrid. The notebooks in which Martí articulated ideas, laid foundations, imagined. In one of these notebooks, published posthumously, all the clues needed to reconstruct the furious polemic he established with "that Karr," who never knew about it. But not necessarily because he was one of those characters whose addiction to his garden should be translated as escapism or isolationism, as abstention from the ways of the world. Far from it, Karr was very active in his era: today he would have been one of those pundits with little substance but a great number of followers.

(After Bernd Stiegler, *Traveling in Place: A History of Armchair Travel*, Chicago: University of Chicago Press, 2013)

• • •

When she opens the door, she sees her boss from behind, squatting as he works, just as she left him yesterday. As if anticipating Mara's question, he explains that without breaking at night it would be impossible for him to continue, no matter how enthusiastic he is, and he quickly moves on to a recitation of his renovation process. If she had seen the shape those horses were in after the flood, the one in the eighties: totally ruined. The whole museum under two meters of water for months. Months, he insists. At that time he was still assisting his father. Things floated by in the most unpredictable directions, garbage bags got snagged on the canopied beds, hats bobbed aimlessly like restless spirits, some pieces took on lives of their own and shot forward like projectiles. Months like that, months under water. And there were the horses, what a mess. Until one day, yes, they exploded. And it's a good thing they did. That absurd structure wasn't right for them. Iron, straw, and plaster had been used for the first taxidermy, an atrocity, indiscriminately monumental, each piece almost five hundred kilos, an impossible weight, the taxidermist emphasizes with unexpected violence, as if knowing his argument is coming too late. They had to mount the horses' hides on top of all that, somehow or other. And they did it badly, of course, very badly. Fortunately, they then exploded. Though she is still looking at him from behind, Mara would swear that the taxidermist is laughing under his breath as he says that last bit. The same thing happened to the mules at the Museo Güiraldes just a few years ago during a different flood, they exploded, he continues, and now a laugh can be heard. Mara wonders if it's only impudence or if his irrepressible laughter might be the effect of some of those chemicals taxidermists use to treat the horses' hides; she knows he uses them even though he doesn't want to reveal which ones. The problem, he says in an emphatic tone directed at the disciple that she is not, was that they did not take measurements of the bodies before flaying them, a basic problem, impossible to fix. They simply built a structure based on a typical specimen of the Criollo race, not specifically on those two horses. Madness, he asserts, and he tilts his head toward them. Mara doesn't turn to look at them. She had enough to deal with the day before when she entered and saw the two horses dismembered, taken apart. The bodies, so to speak, the body-mannequins, were in one corner, the hides spread out in another, and, on his knees on top of those hides, those pelts, the taxidermist was applying his formula like one of those murderers who play with the remains of their victims. There was not, as Mara had assumed all this time, anything like the body they had throughout their life, but rather a mannequin, a dummy. And who knows why that absence perturbs her even more. As if she could tolerate the good intentions implicit in embalming, but not the staging of a taxidermy. No, not that. What was truly disturbing was to realize that all this time she had confused one technique with the other, she had thought of one when she heard the name of the other and vice versa. She had confused the words: she realizes that there was a time when that kind of confusion would have propelled her into a major crisis, and she still doesn't know if this is the kind of transformation that she should also include in the protocol of her detached life. But this is not the moment to think about it, because her boss continues talking about cases and procedures, and if there is something she understands clearly by now it is that the taxidermist's verbosity, which she couldn't tolerate before, which even caused her paroxysms of introspection, has been flipped on its head, has become completely useful to her plans, a mother lode of possibilities. She still doesn't know what form her counterattack will take, but she is certain that whatever it is, it must directly incriminate the taxidermist. Her year of detachment has not been ruined, as she came to believe for a while, it is merely experiencing a hiatus. Incriminating her boss not only guarantees her revenge but also—knowing how local bureaucracies work—a peaceful end to the experiment. Months, years will pass before they find a replacement, if they find one at all, and who knows where she will be by then. The only inconvenience is that from now on she will have to listen to him, because it is clear that nobody is more likely to give her the idea. To go from assistant to undercover spy will force her to give up one of her recently acquired luxuries, that of being permanently heedless of her surroundings, one of the main goals of her experiment. But no need to despair, it's just a hiatus. For a short time, that's all, for a short time she'll have to remain very attentive to everything the taxidermist says in order to hear what she needs to know, or to ask the question, make the appropriate remark at precisely the right moment. To think, this degree of attentiveness to other people's words was among the things she most wanted to leave behind.

• • •

Once in a while, almost in spite of herself, she walks faster. She attempts to imagine the exact moment a horse, a donkey, a polar bear, a leopard, any animal, any taxidermy explodes. Actu-

ally it's probably more of a slow process, an almost imperceptible swelling, which within a few days becomes a deformity,
and then something indefinable, almost menacing, until finally,
yes, it bursts. At one of those moments when you're busy doing something banal—getting a glass of water, brushing your
teeth—something that later becomes meaningful, overvalued,
because there's always the suspicion that if you'd just managed
to change something imperceptible about that banality, then
things would have turned out differently. She's certain that it
can't be something spectacular or cathartic: she figures it has
to be more like an implosion, that the creatures break up from
within. Or they surrender to a crackling of sorts, a collapse. But
she isn't convinced that an explosion as a counterattack is the
right thing. Now she knows she'll commit sabotage, but she
hasn't formulated a plan. She keeps walking, she keeps imagining explosions in spite of herself. She wonders how it came
about in the specific case of those horses, or the mules in the
Museo Güiraldes. She walks faster. Berenice, Berenice, how
long it has been since she's thought of her. She wonders how
she is, if she's still alive. She assumes she is, hopes so, but she
doesn't have any idea what the average lifespan of a mule might
be. Berenice was very young at the time, a baby. A baby who
practically saved her life during those fatal weeks when she was
working in the south of France. A meeting of ministers. Her
then boss had taken ill at the last minute, and they sent her
instead. Mara grew weary of telling her that she was not sufficiently trained for that assignment, that she had never mastered
the subject of terrorism, that she needed to read a lot before
going, that it could end up being a total failure, but her boss
wasn't interested in her excuses. The only thing she did was

mutter comforting prefabricated sentences, sentences that are applicable to any person in any situation. For security reasons, the exact date and place were not specified in advance, so she was required to travel ahead of time in order to be there ready to begin forty-five minutes after they called her on her cell. She was not James Bond, she was simply a novice simultaneous interpreter, she repeated, but her boss opened her mouth only to say, in a litany that seemed to have derived from the use of narcotics, how many people would give anything to spend a few days in the south of France. She had to agree and travel the following day. For more than a week she slept four hours a night, or less. She got up at dawn and downloaded information from the Internet, she wrote to specialists, read newspapers from all over the world, from now and from before; frankly, she was terrified. It was, she is certain, the only time she was afraid because of her job. The other times it was just a matter of adrenaline, or certain levels of rage, but never real fear. When she couldn't stand it any longer, when it seemed to her that there was not a single additional lexical component of geopolitics and terrorism that her mind could retain that day, she wandered around the town, a small town, a few square blocks, to tell the truth, full of English and French retirees who were more or less peasants, more or less reactionaries. By then, she already couldn't stand her work, already by then. Her only solace during those weeks in the French heartland was, first of all, a handful of junkies who had gone there to hang out, people determined to die whenever and however they felt like it. One of them, Melanie, a sixty-something former costume designer, asked her on the first day if she could take a shower at the hotel where Mara was staying. Other days followed that first one.

While she was stuck staring at her computer, her guest spent hours soaking in the bath, punctuating the soak with quick showers for the spa effect, an equation she had no problems with until the day Melanie fell asleep and not only flooded her room but also the one below. Again, a flood, two during the same walk: Mara thinks that someone who plays the lottery would make something of this. She recalls the complaints of the manager, the subtle xenophobia, the still unconfirmed conference, the panic she felt the day they did confirm it, how badly she performed. That same night she called her boss to request an urgent replacement; she didn't care if she had to return what they'd paid her till then, she didn't care if she had to travel back on a container ship. Her boss answered that all this ran contrary to what the minister had said about her work, and that's why she had to stay with him for the committee meetings that would be held the following days, and she was so young and so inexperienced that she believed her and stayed. But by this time she could no longer stand Melanie's whims or her friends' tired jabs at the bourgeoisie, so she avoided all public places and left her room only to take walks along paths that might have still been in the town or already out in the countryside, she wasn't sure. One day she met a local and asked him a few questions; another day, she met a gardener who was working at the house next door to Berenice's. He said that the family of the mule lived in Toulouse, and they visited this, their country house, once a month, sometimes less often now that the girls were older. Berenice spends a lot of time alone, he said. For the rest of her stay, which turned out to be much longer than the seventy-two hours forecast by her boss, Mara brought bread to her every day, and while the mule chewed, she settled accounts with the committee, her boss, the absurd meetings, the world geopolitical situation, and French provincials. She told her that she, Berenice, should join the junkies and rant about all the systems that had reduced animals to the humiliating role of pets. Abandoned pets, to top it off. But not while Mara was still there; she should join them afterwards, because the two of them had a better time alone together.

• • •

She decides to get up and take something for her headache. And eat, eating something always calms her nerves, gives her ideas. She has to think of something; it's hard to believe that she hasn't come up with a plan and it's already been more than a week. She looks to see if there's something left in the box of vegetables Ringo brought her and doesn't find much. She decides to improvise a stew with the bits she has. She chops the vegetables with unnecessary frenzy. While they're cooking, she starts to organize some things that have been piling up on the table for months, but then she reconsiders. Better to sit for a while, settle down in the kitchen. The box of vegetables is still on the floor, almost empty. She sees that it's lined with pages from a magazine: a packaging material that Ringo's father prefers to sterile materials because it seems more authentic, more down-to-earth. She pulls out the pages and reads them, with more urgency than curiosity. A young entrepreneur reveals the secrets of his success. Mara suspects that Ringo's father must have given his son the magazine to motivate him, and his son must have used it to line the boxes without even looking at it. The entrepreneur being interviewed says that he started his project in the family garage, and now he spends his life sitting in airplanes, his company is publicly traded, and he is happy that he can provide jobs for so many people. He says he likes to go out to eat in Silicon Valley because nobody there bothers anybody because they're rich and famous. He says that he's married and has three children and, considering that his family is his pillar of support so that he can do what he does so well, he gives them a lot of quality time. Mara tries to imagine the system: the young entrepreneur taking time in the morning to measure out the quality of the hours while he is breakfasting on something light but also healthful, and deciding which of all the slices is of the highest quality so he can then give those to his wife and children. How does he do it, might there already be a device to measure the quality of time, of life, something that's sold in the kiosks in Silicon Valley? Of course, in those places there aren't any kiosks. She goes outside to get a breath of fresh air in the garden and, for the first time in years, she's dying for a cigarette. But there aren't kiosks open at that time of night in this remote town, either. That sustained discourse about quality and excellence reminds her of the philanthropist at that conference, the one where she chose to carry out her previous sabotage and to thereby say goodbye to her job and her colleagues and her temporary bosses and her promisingly profitable life and the variations on her productive life and achievements and stories about her achievements and her generalized boredom. If she really thinks about it, compared to the statements by the entrepreneur, she prefers those of the taxidermist, because at least he dispenses with euphemisms and openly admits that he is working to improve a race. Her head hurts even more; she's entering one of those invincible and inexorable spirals. She is distracted by a strong odor coming from the kitchen. She goes back inside and sees that her attempt at a stew has been reduced to a dark layer, uniform and dry. She stares at it, as if it were a layer of coffee grounds capable of revealing something to her.

THREE

She picks up her pace, wants to arrive before it gets dark. Now that she has drawn up her sabotage plan, she reviews it: she already knows the schedules of the security guards, she already knows their preferences, what wine they like to drink, she already knows where they keep the key that the taxidermist returns to them every evening and that she will need at a particular time. It's important that she use that key: in this town nobody loses track of what others do, much less if those others are newcomers, and she fears that if she takes the risk of making a copy, a single word from the locksmith will ruin everything. And, given the level of control over all the minutiae that her boss as well as the most introverted security guard have shown, she can't take the risk of removing it for a few hours to make a copy somewhere else. Collecting the basic information she needed to plan each step took a lot less time than she had thought, which shouldn't surprise her after years of devoting herself to a profession that in the final analysis does not consist of speaking two or three or several languages well, as one might think, but rather of grasping quickly what someone really wants to say whenever they say anything. Her pronunciation of the languages she translated wasn't brilliant, she has to admit, but she also has to admit that in the art of perceiving that nucleus, she was infallible. And, since her perceptions were very quick, she had a lot of time shut away in her booth to observe the infinite number of discursive strategies and detours the orators used in order to present that nucleus at precisely the right moment, or to hide it, or to allude to it, or to elude it. She had a lot of time, in short, to understand manipulative discourse. So much so that during the free moments she had in her booth and in hotel rooms and at airports, she began to write her own manual of rhetoric. A manual of manipulative discourse, replete with linguistic examples, prototypes, and digressions. The part about well-documented examples and prototypes, she still believes, is what made everybody so nervous that day she decided to stop translating what was being said at the celebrated summit and instead started to read one of the chapters from her own manual. Though, as it turned out, she was able to read very little, because after exactly seven minutes, the security people removed her by force. Not even a colleague or one of the organizers, but rather the most blatant forces of law and order. A real pity because without a doubt those seven minutes figure among the happiest of her life. Unforgettable the stunned expressions on the faces of well-known journalists, international delegates, key figures, and the few other people who had been allowed into the hall that day when the great philanthropist of the day would finally make a presentation, and not because Mara, instead of translating the first few sentences, chose to read that passage from her manual, the one she'd been writing for all those years, a text that implicated everybody, starting with herself, who was excitedly reading inside her booth, which for the first time ceased to feel like a suffocating box, a chicken coop, and turned into a space ship, a mobile stage, slightly off kilter. Nevertheless, and in spite of how interested some appeared to be, they didn't let her continue, and moreover, afterwards, they went to the trouble of making sure she was expelled from both interpreter associations, the international one and the local one. What they failed to do was assert that she had lost her mind; they found no way to prove that her behavior was the result of a nervous breakdown, so common in her profession, and she preferred it this way despite the advice of her lawyer. It was clear, and continues to be in any case, that her manual errs in the opposite direction: it is the product of balanced, attentive observation; it examines, scrutinizes, dissects, and exposes to what extent conversations and negotiations and debates are vacuous, and to what extent the *isms* of etiquette in international relations are simulacra, and to what extent, independent of the topic being discussed or the pretenses of communication being employed, everything can always be reduced to guessing as quickly as possible what the interlocutor wants in order to move on to vanquish him. At that moment she was truly surprised to what extent the simple description of what was so obvious, even redundant, could generate such incensed reactions. Not anymore: we all know that our hearts beat but not many can tolerate a meticulous description of the tangle of arteries and other mechanisms involved; we all know that on one specific day it will stop beating but we also don't want to know precisely when or how.

• • •

Ringo wants to bring her up-to-date on the last chapters of his escape plan. Mara is making a recipe Luisa gave her and doing so requires every last drop of her concentration. But she has to put her best foot forward: tonight Ringo is going to find out that he's not the only one with plans, and he's also going to find out that she needs his help, his collaboration. In addition to this menu specially prepared to win him over, she needs to make an effort to answer him with something more than onomatopoeias—at this point she knows how much he values her advice. Articulated advice, lines of reasoning, eyewitness accounts, countervailing examples, well-substantiated hypotheses: the conversational demands of her new friend cover a wide spectrum and have undoubtedly been trendsetters of this general tendency to undermine her protocol of silence. But she hasn't failed, she has to remind herself, she is simply experiencing a momentary interruption. Made up of more and more moments. While she waits the twenty minutes stipulated in the recipe, she sits at the counter and finally does ask Ringo a couple of questions, gives him a couple of pieces of advice, and tops it all off with a hunch. The sequence also sounds like a recipe, but she doesn't care. The timer goes off, the twenty minutes have passed. Mara returns to her risotto and, while watching the artichokes change color, she explains to Ringo the motivation and logistics behind her plan to sabotage the taxidermist's work, and she explains the role he will play.

• • •

From the *Notebook*:
One of the obituaries for César Milone lamented the fact that

the doctor carried his secret to the grave. Milone—chief of surgery at the Faculty of Medicine in Rome, a disciple of the renowned embalmer Costanzo Mazzoni, hired in Argentina by the Minister of Public Education Eduardo Wilde, professor of Topographic Anatomy at the Faculty of Medicine in Buenos Aires, chief of dissection on the board of the university, participant in the embalming of Pope Pius IX and Garibaldi— died without revealing any information. Impossible to know the composition of the formula he used to preserve his pieces. Just like Ruysch, the great Dutch anatomist; just like Fragonard, the great French anatomist/artist. "He practiced embalming successfully using a chemical compound the ingredients of which he kept secret." That's what the obituary for Milone, published on September 30, 1904, said. Why carry the secret all that way? Megalomania? Stinginess? Likely more of an occupational hazard that leads one to not believe in death, neither one's own nor that of others. Embalmers have the tics of children: they believe in eternity, they converse with those very serious figurines they see in their display cabinets, they don't want to share their dolls. They preserve corpses, they preserve knowledge. They keep, hold, hide, retain: they are terrified children. Just then, at Milone's death, the Gutiérrez brothers decided to counteract all that mystery and wage war from their newspaper, *La Patria Argentina*. Buenos Aires was under siege by the plague, and cremation not embalming was required; the corpses needed to be gotten rid of to prevent them from spreading the disease post mortem. They asserted something to that effect in their newspaper while cholera and the yellow plague wreaked havoc on the city and while the Catholic sectors were advocating for the preservation of corpses. A few months after the first official cremation in Buenos Aires, *La Patria Argentina* recommended a continuation of this practice rather than burial. And embalming, even less, which is what Dr. César Milone, along with his associate, Polidoro Segers, was doing. First target of the Gutiérrez brothers: Segers's text—promulgated by his company with headquarters at Lavalle 736, along with affordable prices for any mortal—that defines embalming as the perfect synthesis between hygienic practices and religious beliefs, a practice that neither spreads disease nor pitches our loved ones into the flames. Next target: the exhibit of Segers's embalmed pieces in the Buenos Aires Amphitheater. The newspaper of the Gutiérrez brothers suggested they analyze the formula used in that exhibition as a final flourish against the embalmer. They looked for, asked, insisted, and hunted until they found their informant. Eduardo Retienne, the chemist who prepared the chemicals for Segers, confirmed to them that it was neither the preparation used by Sucquet, so widely employed in this region, nor the one used by Lemaire, nor the one used by Gannal nor by Dupré; instead, Segers used Jean Wickersheimer's formula, which he imported from Berlin and which promised, as opposed to the previous preparations, to maintain flexibility and color. Retienne knew because he was the one, following Wickersheimer's formula word-for-word, who mixed one hundred parts alum, twenty-five parts table salt, twelve parts potassium nitrate, sixty parts potash, and ten parts arsenic acid in three thousand parts boiling water.

(After Irina Podgorny, "*Recuerden que están muertos*" [Remember that they are dead], in *Espacios y cuerpos en la Argentina del siglo XIX y comienzos del XX*, Buenos Aires: Ediciones de la Biblioteca National/Teseo, 2009.)

• • •

Her boss, sitting on one of those stools used by meditators or in nursery schools, is working on Mancha's left ankle, adding hairs onto the hides that he has finished restoring. Light enters through the upper window of the cabinet. Mara figures that this is why the fur has that special sheen and thinks again about the suicidal bird who never showed up again. The taxidermist looks more serious than usual. She assumes it's because of the phase of the work, the concentration required. All the better: this afternoon Mara has planned to somehow look once again through all the papers and files; it's difficult for her to believe that the chemical formula the taxidermist uses on the hides exists only in his head. Not even in his father's, he assured her a few days ago, because it's been some time since they took different paths and began to follow different protocols. And he doesn't use a computer, so he doesn't run the risk of somebody stealing random data or a password in an attempt to discover it. Deplorable, unacceptable, unbelievable the state those horses were in, he now says, a few minutes after seeing her. Luckily, at least, that first deplorable taxidermy was done in winter. The coat in winter is longer so it has a greater chance of lasting and protecting the hides. Pure luck, or divine intervention. If it weren't for that, they would have also had to redo the horses' hides, the only truly original part of Mancha and Gato that remains. If it weren't for that intervention, if it weren't for that winter, not the slightest trace would have been left of this identity that he is now bringing back to life. Not the slightest trace. At most they'd have a couple of wrapped polyurethane dolls. But that's not it, this is not a toy factory, gentlemen; this is an art, a higher form of art, so much higher that it is capable of restoring life. He gets up from his stool and starts to pace back and forth. This startles Mara, but she manages to conceal it. She continues to organize the items on the table/desk, just as is stipulated in the week's work schedule. Nails, nails, who could have guessed that in these hides that are now becoming what they were before, somebody would have stuck so many nails, he says, and he keeps pacing around as if he were in a trance, or sleepwalking. Mara puts aside the papers where she believes she can find part of what she is looking for, some new clue at least, then goes back to looking through them more carefully as soon as her boss returns to his stool. For her sabotage she doesn't need to find the complete formula; knowing the ingredients, or at least some of the ingredients, is enough. It's important, very important, her boss warns her, not to forget to call back the fur bank, because if he doesn't receive that material by next week, he'll be in trouble. Now, call right now, and he sits back down. He only deals with the best fur banks, he insists, now almost talking to himself. From what Mara manages to see, he is adding new hairs to the already treated hides. She tries to find the cordless phone, which, she is certain, must be somewhere on that table, but instead her hand happens upon a cold, inscrutable object, a cold object that looks at her, or something like that. A glass eye, she thinks. Yes, Gato's eye, the taxidermist explains, and this time he does perceive how she startles. In fact, he is particularly concerned because the next order should also include the hair he needs to reconstruct the eyelashes. Those ocular prostheses belong to the first taxidermy, the one done in the forties, he adds, parts that have historical value in themselves, and from there he launches into another episode of verbosity, though in this particular case Mara doesn't listen to him because it seems the perfect moment to look over the papers more thoroughly. She employs her skill at reading upside down, acquired after years in her profession. Again, nothing. She has the impression that the loose eye is watching her. She looks over at the taxidermist and notices that his loquacity does not interfere in the slightest with the steady hand he needs for this very meticulous stage of his work. She calls the fur bank and then pretends to keep organizing things while she waits for the right moment to ask the right question.

• • •

Luisa arrives late at the agreed-upon street corner and as soon as they greet each other she starts to tell Mara a story that Mara has difficulty focusing on. She manages to understand only that it has something to do with a couple of colleagues she doesn't know and a conference that is being organized. She should pay attention: the activities at the museum in the next few days could determine the success or failure of her plan. They walk toward Luisa's house, where Luisa has arranged for her to meet Honoria. The streets are empty, not even stray dogs go out at this time of day. They walk by one of those shop windows where a shopkeeper has dressed a manikin with such painstaking care that this is the only thing one notices, not the garments themselves. According to what Mara was finally able to wheedle out of her boss, in addition to the funds for the restoration of the horses donated by the Association, an insurance company had demanded that the formula used for the restoration cease to be the exclusive secret of the taxidermist and be recorded in some other place in order to guarantee that the excellence of the final product be protected in case of any personal mishap. It had been difficult, in these days of airborne information, to fight to not upload or share; it had been difficult, he repeated, but he had finally managed to reach an agreement that the only other place his formula would be stored was in a safe in the museum library. The taxidermist said this with derision. Mara heard it with gratitude. And then, without even a hint of pressure, Luisa arranged a meeting with her aunt. Honoria seemed key not only because of her access to the information in the library but also because of her animus toward the museum's mythos, which she thought she perceived that day at her gathering, because of her predisposition to put up a fight.

• • •

From the *Notebook*:
A fox smoking a water pipe, a flying cat, another cat as a coffee table, a mouse playing the guitar, two squirrel monkeys having sex, a lamb giving birth to a duck, a meditating monkey, a cat with the front legs of a large bird, maybe a flamingo's. Taxidermies of this sort gathered together on a website. So far, a joke, a wink at the bizarre, I suppose. Unremarkable. There are others, however, in and among the photos in this sensationalist line: a polar bear with a smashed head, a dog with the facial expression of a lost lunatic, a cat with electrified ears, a cross-eyed monkey, a variety of pets with twisted limbs and lolling tongues, as if they'd had a stroke from which they've never recovered. From a bad joke we move on to what goes wrong. Precisely this, the power of what goes wrong, this must be what gener-

ates a certain amount of discomfort as I scroll through these other pictures. There is no intentionality, just error. But error isn't the point, either. It's the unexpected course of events. Not that, either. Rather the wretched course of events. Things went well until an expression turned into a grimace, a sneer, and there was no turning back. The discomfort settled in, froze. Not discomfort: wretchedness. Right when it seemed as if a bounty of virtues had settled in forever—the ultimate goal of taxidermy—something interfered, erased the bounty, and, also, forever, installed the grimace, the oppression, the panic, the wretchedness. What went wrong: eternally paralyzed. Taxidermies that defy all credos, all disciplines, all self-help narratives: sometimes things go wrong forever, sometimes there's no possible fix. That's what some of these taxidermies are saying, even if they are disguised as a joke.

(After the website "Badly Stuffed Animals.")

• • •

It happens in spring, one of her colleagues said during lunch. With hot weather on the horizon, people pick up the "microtourism" circuit, which includes the museum, that's why there are so many more visitors this weekend. The boss joined them at that lunch to beg heartily for them to remember to be particularly alert over the next few days, to not leave their posts, to not get distracted; they know, she underscored, the risks involved when the museum is full of visitors, they've even had to suffer the consequences: thefts, damaged pieces, they know exactly what she's talking about; and then, before sitting to eat her meal that was already getting cold, she added that during the week they would still have time to get back to that little sweater they were knitting for their child or grandchild, and catch up on the latest news about whatever and whoever, but please, for these few days focus on keeping watch, which implies also circulating around their respective rooms, not just sitting there. Precisely today, however, and in a way that hasn't happened to her in a long time, the lumbar syndrome has taken hold of Mara, keeping her captive. She wouldn't trade that contact with the chair for anything. She is fortunate to be in the Transportation Room, she has to admit: anybody can stuff a cane or a hairpin or a locket or even a hat under their coat, but nobody is going to steal, undetected, a snowplow or the sailboat that broke the world record for sailing solo around the world. And if they do, Mara will have no choice but to congratulate them. Honoria's response to her plan has affected her more than it should have, she must admit, though she still can't figure out exactly why, why so much. More than a week has already passed since that encounter at her house, and she still hasn't reacted, she still can't emerge from a combined state of astonishment, rage, and bemusement. Honoria welcomed her into her husband's office and there, barricaded in that ancient, phantasmagorical stage set, she responded with a proclamation to Mara's simple request that one of these days, any day that she goes to pick up or leave some work materials in the museum library, Honoria do her best to find out the combination of the safe and, perhaps that same day, open it and copy down the taxidermist's secret formula. The trust Mara had placed in her before hearing her response, before even suspecting that proclamation, was so great that she'd already shared with her the specifics of her plan, she'd already told her that she would use the taxidermist's formula to destroy the recently restored horses the night before the opening of the big exhibition, to incriminate him for bad praxis, to humiliate him and all his minions, and, most importantly, to be able to carry on with her life, with her experiment. Her prior trust was so great that she even spoke to her of her detached life experiment that afternoon in that ancient office, and she even spoke at length about the series of events that had inspired her, about the conference, her expulsion, the prohibition against her working in her profession, and above all the fatigue, the existential hangover, the need to take some distance from the world's redundancy. A tactical distance at least, a limited escape in order to redefine her strategy, she remembers having said because it was only then, with that sentence, she remembers clearly, that Honoria looked up from the papers she had continued to work on while she had been talking. Not a tactical distance, a tactical error, she said. A classic tactical error, she repeated, with that hoarse voice of a smoker that still, whatever detractors of smoking might say, adds legitimacy to assertions. Maybe that's where Mara's rage comes from, from her trust that was based on a mistaken intuition, or rather, a mistaken reading of Honoria's work on Udaondo's archives, where Mara believed she saw a plan to posthumously checkmate the feudal lord. Solitary acts like that have no meaning, she continued. Or rather, began. The problem with isolated acts like the one Mara is planning and like so many others have planned before her, Honoria said, is that in the end they serve only to weaken the movement, to disrupt it. Such actions undermine the foundations of the combat-ready brigades on which one can pin serious hopes. Individual resistance is nothing but an expression of despair, a lack of faith, unreliable prating, a bourgeois gesture, which is part and parcel of the logic of the enthusiasm of intellectuals, their hysteria, their inability to carry through with a firm and dogged labor. The thing is, she, Mara, and all those who think and act as she does, worship spontaneity instead of channeling their indignation and revolutionary energy into an organization that is capable of uniting their forces and training them to be prepared when the decisive battle arrives. It's not a simple task, but it is worthwhile to remember Marx's words, which so often and with so little success have recently been quoted, and affirm that "every step of *real* movement is more important than dozens" of attacks and individual acts of resistance. It's important that she understand, know how to distinguish, differentiate. Know how to wait. Tactics shouldn't be a reaction to the spontaneity of an attack but rather to the organization of united forces. Spontaneous outbursts by solo actors and even the mob always run the risk of going astray, she can assure her. That's the mistake, that's the threat implicit in planning to act outside of an organization that organizes, educates, and unites. She doesn't doubt her good intentions, Honoria added, calling forth a prosody that sounded to Mara vaguely maternal, far be it from her to want to deny the bravery of acts carried out with heroism, no matter how solitary they are, but it's her duty to warn her against employing such a method in the current situation. She doesn't doubt her good intentions, but Mara should know that the road to hell is paved with good intentions.

• • •

They order the usual, the waiter says *the usual*. Luisa mentions that today is actually the anniversary of the death of her mother.

A heart attack in the middle of the night, without any warning whatsoever. Without time to say goodbye, finish any conversations, no time for anything. Then she stares out the window. Mara mutters the beginning of several clichés but doesn't finish any of them. Then, without knowing how, or rather, giving in to the loquacity that has recently only accentuated the holding pattern she finds herself in, she begins to tell the story of a movie she saw a long time ago. It takes place in a cold and sparsely populated country, somewhere in Alaska, she thinks. A woman dies in a snowstorm, the rescuers can't find her, her family waits for her in vain for days. Until one morning, many months later, while walking to town, one of her sons finds her. His mother is covered with a thin layer of snow, but in spite of how much time has passed, she is intact, identical, as if she were merely sleeping. This son, who happens to be an oddball, the one who has always felt a little uncomfortable in his family, decides not to tell anybody. At least initially, or so it seems, at least until he has had enough time to have those conversations that we always believe have been left hanging when our loved ones die. He doesn't mention anything to anybody, and every night before going to sleep he jots down a list of questions, accusations, mysteries, confessions: a sort of "collected letters" from a son who holds nothing back. And in the morning, after the family breakfast, he sneaks out to the gully where his mother's corpse is, but when he wants to mention one of those issues, read one of his own paragraphs, he manages only to stammer out some syllables and can't even formulate a single sentence. His mother looks at him serenely, sunk in the sweet dreams that come to those who freeze to death, or so they say. The movie reaches points of cruelty and absurdity that can only be tolerated with outbursts of laughter, or at least that's what happened to her, Mara says, and then she suddenly repents, the sentence sounds so harsh. She's not used to talking to Luisa, only listening to her. She goes to the bathroom and splashes water on her face. When she returns, Luisa says that she's worried about what happened with her aunt. If she'd had any inkling that she'd react the way she did, she never would have set up that meeting, and she asks Mara to please forgive her. She should keep in mind that Honoria is over seventy and moreover her plan of sabotage, if she'll forgive her, is not precisely the kind of thing that wins people over just by being spelled out. Suddenly Mara sees her as an adult, without any connection to the Luisa she knows. She has already spoken with her aunt, Luisa adds, and she can vouch for her that nothing incriminating will ever come out of her mouth. She even believes that deep down, and even if it implies a betrayal of her Leninist convictions, Honoria hopes her plan will work. Mara abstains from mentioning the shock her aunt caused her in her mausoleum, speaking like a reincarnation, a ventriloquist's doll, not of her husband, as she assumed at first, but rather of some kind of composite figure assembled from all the books that she keeps on those endless, old, frozen shelves. There's something about Honoria that's similar to an embalmed piece, she thinks, but this time she can't follow the course of her own meandering thoughts because Luisa is giving her some kind of signal. She has also spoken to people in the museum, she says, a bit bluntly, as if to highlight her irritation at having to put up with another one of those introspective lapses that Mara always thought were imperceptible to others. She says she took it upon herself to find people who had more information about the opening of the exhibition being planned for December and, as far as she understands, it will be in part an homage to the horses, in part a family celebration, and in large part a fundraiser. It seems like it's really about getting a pharmaceutical company to commit to fund not only this exhibit but also a section of the museum, making it a permanent donor. She doesn't remember the name of the company, but she's sure that it's important; they're the ones who recently cloned a Criollo horse, it appeared in all the newspapers, they told her. She figures that they'll all speak on the day of the opening, and they will even hire some historian to tell the in-depth story of the intimate connection between those two heroic examples, now restored, and the new generation of clones. Mara looks at her, flustered by the results of the inquiry, and reviews the definition of one type of silence in her manual of rhetoric, the third one: "Complacent silence consists not only of devoting oneself to listening to those one is trying to please but also of giving them signs of the pleasure we take in their conversation and their behavior, whereby the looks, the expressions, everything compensates for the lack of words that offer praise." She cannot help wondering once again how it is possible to come to love someone so much in so little time.

· · ·

From the *Notebook*:
A woman used to clean a laboratory at the Faculty of Agronomy in Buenos Aires. She was on the janitorial staff, not part of the team of researchers. She thought that the liquid she found in one of the many receptacles was stagnant water and threw it out, but she was wrong: it was embryos in formaldehyde

that the scientists had been working with for more than two months. From those embryos should have been born at least one clone of a famous polo player's best mare, which would then be auctioned off, as had been done not long before with another clone, which sold to an also famous tennis player for eight hundred thousand dollars. But that other clone was raised in the United States, where cleaning ladies have to sign a piece of paper that says they will be burned at the stake if they move a single item from where they find it. What price did that cleaning lady have to pay for throwing out the clones in the Faculty of Agronomy in Buenos Aires? Was she reprimanded, fired? Deported because she was Paraguayan? Sued, her assets seized? But what—what things, what assets—can be seized from a Paraguayan or an Argentinean cleaning lady? Can a cleaning lady be a character in one of those screenplays that revolve around the value of a single life? Eight hundred thousand dollars for the clone, twenty-five million dollars for the best race horse in the world. That was the equation in 2010, when the first cloned Criollo horse was born in Argentina. BS Ñandubay Bicentenario was his name. An impossible name for a pet but not for the sire of horses that will perform well in the most important races. A laboratory at a California university certified that the genes were identical, that the clone had all the virtues of the sire, the great champion Ñandubay, except that BS Ñandubay Bicentenario is not castrated so can better compete in those races and also sire other specimen who will be castrated and will compete and perform well. The other names come from his other parents: a large pharmaceutical company and the State. BS is the acronym of the first and Bicentenario is the historical moment to be memorialized by the Ministry of Science and Technolo-

MARÍA SONIA CRISTOFF

gy. The first celebrates the ability to preserve the genetic capital of the clone and the second celebrates its ability to function as a symbol of a country that does not forget its traditions but is also innovative and technologically advanced. Company and State united once again; in this case, around a project to improve lives. Appraised lives, not just any life.

(After Gonzalo Figueroa, *El joven que clona caballos* ["The young man who clones horses"], *Brando* magazine, Buenos Aires, January 2011.)

• • •

Two things surprise her as soon as her eyes adjust to the dim light in the workshop: Gato's eye now inserted into his body and adorned with perfect, lush eyelashes, eyelashes like those of a high-fashion model; and her work stool occupied by the taxidermist's wife. Her boss tells her that as soon as she puts down her things she should start setting up the camera to take a few shots he'll soon specify. This is precisely the right moment, he explains, the key moment when whole sections of the animal still coexist, sections that bear witness to the situation that required his intervention along with others where one can see the soothing effect of his work, his golden touch. In three days there will be no further vestiges of the defects, in three days his work will begin the transition into its final stage, and the ensemble will be on its way to beauty, perfection, he should say. But beware, it is very important to not remove all vestiges of the past. Here there is art, here there is science, and here there is great respect for the original. Being immersed in a taxidermy always means coming in contact with the spirit of the era, establishing a connection with the breath that gave life to the being one is working with, whether human or animal. And to do that, one must dive deep, keep abreast of things, stay focused. He has spent many sleepless nights during that process, Talvikki here can attest to that, he says, pointing to his wife. For him it is, without a doubt, the most demanding stage of his work, the most mystical even, because it means forging a point of entry into a dimension where you recover a light, an unnameable flame, and you plant it in this world again. That is not the same as churning out more specimens, identical to the previous ones. Not in the least. It's not true that the aura is lost, those are crass theories of haunted minds. He insists that there are multiple ways of proving that none of it is lost. And Talvikki can, too, even though she sometimes refuses to admit it. Just as she is about to take the fifth photograph her boss has requested, Mara looks at his wife, but she doesn't see any sign at all that she feels she is being referred to. Or anything else. Mara figures she must always be like that: he talks, babbles on and on, explains and justifies, while she gives herself over entirely to her Nordic daydreams. Mara has no doubt about that. On the other hand, as she is leaving once the day's session is over, she cannot be absolutely certain that she saw from Talvikki a knowing look as she said goodbye, or if it was only in her own head.

• • •

She unwraps the bottles of wine she carried hidden in her backpack and places them in the center of the table, like trophies. There is something childlike in the delighted reaction of the two security guards. The previous day she stopped by to see them, and before much was said they had already invited her to join them for a barbeque under the trees. She suggested post-poning it till today, even though it's not ideal for her plans, because now, during this momentary hiatus in her experiment, she can't help but allow certain habits of her past life to seep back in, such as scheduling, organizing things ahead of time. She always assumed that in her new life she would be freed from this, not by giving herself over to improvisation but by dispensing with plans altogether. Nothing to schedule, nothing to accept. And she still thinks this, except now she must pass through this phase, get past this interruption, defeat it, subdue it. To think that the other day Honoria accused her of giving in to spontaneity. Spontaneity? Mara? The truth is, she takes it as a compliment: only inside her booth did she know anything about that, but outside of it, never. The one tending the grill asks his friend, who has barely opened his mouth since Mara arrived, to set the table and make sure not to forget anything. Then he employs a ceremonious sentence to announce that, in this heat, he's going to have to remove his shirt. Mara sees that he's wearing a plastic cross on his surprisingly hairless chest. As he proceeds through the steps he calls "the rituals of the grill master," he tells stories of his life at the police academy. Mara assumes that ever since he was young he has been one of those extroverted people, capable of converting friendliness into a means of always doing what he wants. He seems happy with life, or something of the sort. The other one stays a ways away, near the table with the wobbly legs, deep in thought. They make one of those couples that perfectly complement each other. While the extrovert keeps telling stories, Mara has a perfect line of sight to the other one, so she can watch without appearing intrusive. There's something about him that makes her distrust him, something that perfectly matches the stereotype of the Buenos Aires policeman. He's retired, they told her yesterday. Actually, the other one told her, the hairless one, who is now explaining in detail about the small business he set up with his brother-in-law to sell spare parts to all the people who've recently moved to this town as a result of the security situation, even though as far as he's concerned they're just a bunch of rich folks who are impossible to understand. They leave behind their offices, their jobs, and they come here to start from scratch. That's a security situation for you, he laughs. It's nuts, but he's happy, he's got no complaints at all. Thanks to them he bought a new car at the beginning of the year. And the successes pile up, and apparently include his sons and his nephews, who turn out to be the sons of his partner. Mara tastes a bite of what he offers her and calms down. She has just learned that when they throw her out of the museum for neglecting her duties she'll have another job to support herself.

• • •

The river stinks. Mara, however, continues walking along its banks. She can't avoid it. As she walks she kicks the garbage left behind after a weekend of microtourism; it feels therapeutic, and she needs that. The few people who cross her path look at her as if she were crazy. On Mondays, this place looks like the movie set of a retro catastrophe movie, images of the apocalypse as imagined in the fifties. The kiosks and shops are closed, but you can see what they have inside. Her favorite is one that has games for children, almost all based on predictable riddles or some other kind of basic skills tests, and that give prizes that nobody would think of as prizes: plastic dolls, a variety of sweets, hats with visors, and a badly damaged ball, which nobody ever wins, most likely by design. She wonders what those kids, dragged along on microtourism vacations after being connected to their cybernetic entertainment all week, think about these games. They must experience it as time travel, or like one of those history programs with those snooty announcers shown on the documentary channels. She looks at this devastation, the sour aftertaste of cheap consumerism, pieces of which she keeps kicking as she goes, which float in the water, and suddenly she remembers the face the museum director pulled a few days ago when she called a meeting of the entire staff to talk to them about the importance of the fast-approaching exhibition and to make clear to them what is expected of them; but she had not finished her sentence when somebody raised their hand and asked if anybody had thought about cleaning up the river for that day of the homage and exhibition. Few times had she seen so much discomfort in one face. Perhaps because the question, she's certain, had been asked with total innocence.

• • •

During the second rehearsal, she deliberately slowed down each movement; she's planning to carry out her sabotage late at night, and she knows that this, in addition to the need for stealth, will undoubtedly slow her down. Now she knows it, she just proved it. She has studied and timed every step but she still doesn't know what chemicals to use to trash those horses, destroy them. Impossible to find at least one of the components of that ridiculous formula, now she understands why the taxidermist didn't want specialized assistants. Definitely impossible, no matter how much she's tried. This place, without a doubt, is totally destroying her ability to guess what another person is thinking. To think that for years this was the key to what they called her brilliant career, the reason they hired her for the most interesting and highly paid conferences. It's true, if she focused on what someone was saying, she could almost guess word for word what would come next. Or not exactly, but the main idea, at least, which is what counts. Shut away in her booth, she would go into a kind of trance, and then she'd listen and guess at the same time or grasp it telepathically in advance or it was dictated to her from another world, she never bothered to find out how it worked for her, but it did. On a few occasions, this gift frightened her, she'd feel a kind of vertigo. But apparently she's not so infallible anymore, all her strategies at industrial espionage have failed. She has no intention of giving up on her plans because of this, but she really regrets it: using at least one of the components of the formula for the sabotage was a more direct, more efficient means of incriminating the taxidermist. All she had to do was inject a larger dose into the recently restored horses, an exorbitant dose, something that would really destroy his work and that could not be ascribed to anything other than bad praxis. No other suspects. She'll carry out her sabotage with a different product, soon she'll figure out which. She gets up from her chair and walks back again to the ticket window, but there's nothing new. She's been waiting almost two hours for a bus that will take her back home. Over the loudspeakers they said that the road to her town is closed, the company considers it preferable for the passengers to wait here at the station until it opens up, rather than on the road, then no further announcements. And nobody has asked any questions after that shrill announcement. Everybody here seems to surpass her in spades when it comes to the practice of a detached life, which she didn't achieve, as it turned out. For now, at least. That man she always sees when she takes the bus back, for example, he was walking toward the platforms when he heard the announcement, then he looked at his watch, grabbed a newspaper that someone had left on a rickety chair who knows when, and he's been sitting there ever since. He's still reading it. A newspaper with probably fewer than thirty pages. Mara could swear that the frequent passenger has not looked at his watch again the whole time. She decides to go outside to get a little fresh air even though the afternoon heat doesn't feel very inviting. At that very moment she sees the taxidermist's wife approaching with her ethereal stride. She appears near the platforms, where Mara is waiting, then walks over to the ticket window. While waiting to be helped, she looks disconsolately toward the inside of the station, where the number of people and bags and stray dogs has been increasing throughout the afternoon. Someone comes to the window, and Talvikki appears to ask something, something she's worried about. Then she returns to the area near the platforms and lights a cigarette. Mara gets up and greets her with all the restraint she can summon. They exchange a few pleasantries about the closure, the possible reasons for it—idle comments. Talvikki keeps staring at the platforms, as if any second the TGV in Paris will arrive rather than a ramshackle bus in the middle of the province of Buenos Aires. Mara can't determine if it's the bother of having to talk to her or some other kind of anxiety that gives the woman that fixed expression of being elsewhere, of escape. On the other hand, another perception is quickly becoming a certainty, a kind of insight that assaults her there among the bags and the loudspeakers and the stray dogs: this woman could be the person who finally helps her carry out her task; she has to know something, even if not the complete formula, at least some of its components. Based on what Luisa said, she often buys materials for her husband. Mara asks some casual questions, engaging in one of those conversational throat-clearings she has become so adept at. The key is to establish the right tone from the beginning, which she figures she can still do. Then it's simply a matter of letting the other talk and remaining sufficiently alert so as to grasp what she needs at precisely the right time. Talvikki says that she was born in Finland, and she appears to be less eager to talk about her husband's work than her own. Studies in fine arts at the Aalto-yliopisto in Helsinki, some time in academia, a few shows of her work, other countries, more shows, other cities, a lot more shows, until she met the taxidermist, and she was tempted by the idea of coming here. She looks at her watch, looks back at the platforms. It was because of her husband, or rather, his work. She met him when he was restoring pieces at the museum in Antwerp, where she was conducting research. While she watched him obsess over the perfect form, over attaining the original or even surpassing it, she couldn't help but focus on everything that was thrown out during every taxidermy. The guts, the organs, the bones, the sinews, the fragments of skin. She stopped seeing them as what they were, and she started to see them as raw material, a strange type of material: something in constant oscillation between life and death. That's the line she's working in, one could say. She lights another cigarette and looks again toward the platforms. Mara is almost more surprised than excited about this moment of unexpected extroversion, but she doesn't lose focus. Talvikki tells her that she came to the station because she's waiting for material that should have arrived from Buenos Aires. Polyester resin, to be precise. She uses it to make sculptures out of bones. In this case, bones from a couple of pumas her husband is taxidermizing at the moment, one of those private orders that pay really well, not like at the museum. Hunters, most of his clients are hunters who decide one day they want to keep a certain piece as a trophy. Who knows why. There are a lot more people with fetishes than you'd think, she says, and she stubs out on the frame of an iron door what must be her seventh cigarette since she started waiting. Whatever comes between her and her work, she explains, makes her very nervous.

• • •

Mara looks at the bed where she is supposedly going to spend the night, and she is reminded of that Pygmy tribe she visited in Burundi. A bit because of its size, another bit because of the sorry state of the room in general. There's a little window with the blinds down, but she doesn't feel like raising them. One night, it's for just one night, she repeats to herself, but even so she doesn't dare put down her backpack, or sit down. Something like dejection is hovering. And here, no Pygmy children will come to sing her those hypnotic songs. She goes to the bathroom: something tells her that if she does the first thing she always does when she enters a hotel room she'll be able to convince herself that she is in a hotel room. Leaning against the tiles is a rubber floor squeegee that she can't avoid seeing as a Giacometti figure, in tears. She regrets not having walked home. Now it's too late, much too late. She goes back to the bathroom to splash water on her face, but this time she doesn't turn on the light. If she thinks about it, she should be grateful. She would never have been able to have a one-on-one conversation with Talvikki if it hadn't been for that bus that never showed up. It must have been ten o'clock when the same loudspeakers that had announced the delay announced the cancellation of service, and the two of them were still talking. Talvikki wanted to know when the next bus would come, she'd run out of resin at the most important moment. Mara's help deciphering some of those blurry shapes behind the dirty ticket window in the terminal was crucial. They left the station together, on foot. She'd spent days and days chopping up the bones of one of the pumas, Talvikki said, remaining focused so she could summon up all the patience that work requires, and now, right when she could dig into the best phase of her work—mixing the remains with the resin—the material doesn't arrive. Mara asked her a technical question in order to segue out of a zone that could devolve, she intuited, into a ritornello with no exit, and, even worse, with no results. Talvikki asked her to call her Tal, as her friends call her, which means her husband and the woman who comes to clean the house three times a week, because the truth is she doesn't talk to anybody else in this town. And then she described how she cuts the bones into very thin slices with an electric saw, just like a good chef, she specified, and then she chops them up, which is what she had been doing for the last few days. It's a somewhat tense process, which requires a lot of patience. A lot. Some of her colleagues delegate that kind of work to assistants, but she never does. She puts on good music and gets to work. She takes it as a kind of meditation, a way to get into the groove, so to speak. In fact, it's precisely during that stage of the work that she's managed to feel most clearly, most palpably, the ambivalence between life and death. She's just run out of cigarettes, she realizes as she pats the pockets of her designer jacket. She can't believe days like this, she just can't believe them. Mara assures her that there must be someplace open at that time of night, she can go with her, and she continues with her questions, which sound casual. She's always worked in a similar line, from the beginning, Talvikki says, since her first piece. The one she made when she was a kid, when her brother died. Her only brother, the love of her life. A ski accident: an incomprehensible sport. When his body arrived in Helsinki, her parents decided to cremate him. And that's what they did, without even holding a wake, and that same night, after the ceremony, they went to bed early, to be as rested as possible the following day when they were going to travel to the seaside, to a little town to the north, where they always spent their summers, to spread his ashes. In fact, that night and all of the following nights, her parents went to bed early, almost always without feeding her dinner. The truth is that she doesn't know why she's remembering that now, precisely now. Because she can't work, because the resin didn't come, because she doesn't have cigarettes. Anyway, the truth is, in her most recurrent memory of childhood she is standing in front of an open refrigerator, the light dim, trying to decide what she can throw together to make a decent dinner. But that night, the night her brother was cremated, she didn't have that problem. She looked in her notebooks for a cookie recipe that she'd learned in school a while before and got started. The ashes of her brother and the flour mixed together perfectly, to this day she doesn't understand how her parents weren't capable of recognizing it. Not that, and not the act of love contained in those cookies. Her only brother, her only family. That's more or less how she works now. Except she has to be very careful with the resin that didn't arrive today, and that she hopes will arrive tomorrow, because it's highly toxic. Many artists have died because they didn't know that. She doesn't even touch it; she wears a suit, kind of like an astronaut's, when she works with it. She does the same thing to handle the formulas she uses to reduce the animal remains—the organs, the paws, the pieces of skin that her husband discards. She always makes sure they're unrecognizable, turned into a gelatin, a powder, a liquid; she does make sure something latent of the animal remains in every one of her works, even if perfectly camouflaged, transformed into indiscernible particles. Mara remembers feeling a chill in her teeth at that point in the story, and she feels it again now, at that very moment, sitting on the bed in that scruffy hotel room and clinging to her backpack. Talvikki Ranta—she made sure to make a mental note of her whole name. She goes down to the bar, which is also reception. They not only have a sandwich but also an internet connection on the computer on one of the tables in the back. First she answers a few emails, the indispensable ones, as she has been doing since she got to this place. Fortunately, with time, their numbers have dwindled; it's been a while now since she stopped feeling, as she had at first, like a screenwriter, simultaneously following several strands of a story, because in order to justify her year of absence without alarming anybody, she told her friends one thing, her family another, and a few colleagues yet another, and so on. For a long time she was struggling to credibly maintain a series of jobs in remote places, a family emergency, and a contagious disease. Anything was preferable to raising an alarm with her absence, even though it was her absence that they were so used to. Once the last of the emails is finished, she looks to see if Talvikki exists in cyberspace. She scans several of the top hits. She puts down the sandwich and starts to read one in particular, an interview she did with a London magazine about her show at the Biennale of Saõ Paulo. Mara has the impression that when she mentions the South American animals she works with, Talvikki includes her husband on the list.

• • •

From the *Notebook*:
Marion receives a transfusion of horse blood. But she doesn't go into shock or fall ill because Marion isn't one of those undocumented women who offer themselves for risky medical trials in order to pay the rent or obtain a passport; she's a French artist who prepared for this long in advance. For months, under the supervision of a Swiss pharmaceutical company, she was injected with small doses of horse immunoglobulin until those antibodies were able to withstand her own organism's defense systems, enter her bloodstream, and, as a result of that synthesis, take effect in her body without making it burst. That's why today, in this aesthetically antiseptic operating room set up in the gallery in Ljubljana where she is presenting her performance, she can receive the blood with so much glamour, wrapped entirely in black and raised on heels that are in fact prostheses in

the shape of equine hooves. She is accompanied by the horse-blood donor, also black, visibly averse to all the ceremony. Hyper-powerful, hypersensitive, hyper-nervous, a superhuman: so Marion said she felt after the experiment. She also said that her piece is a denunciation of the anthropocentrism implicit in the genetic manipulations animal and plant species are subjected to. The old misstep of including social critique in a piece that is supposed to be avant-garde. "May the Horse Live in Me," is the literal translation of the title Marion and Benoît Mangin, her partner, assigned to the piece. "Get Off Your High Horse," is what they should have called it, I think, as I get lost in the small streets of this impossible city.

(After *Que le Cheval Vive en Moi*, performance piece by the duo Art Orienté Objet, Ljubljana, Kapelica Gallery, 2011.)

• • •

Every time she eats lunch there, in the room where her colleagues usually eat lunch, she can't help but be reminded of all the common spaces of the condemned: dining rooms in hospitals, military barracks, offices, boarding schools. The smell of food prepared for many, the clanking of metal trays, the understory murmurs, a combination of all those things. She always thought that the act of feeding oneself, which is very different from eating, should be private. And in this room, where the museum employees gather, that opinion has only gained strength. In any case, she goes there rarely, as infrequently as possible. She was well trained in her previous life: other than breakfast, whenever she could she would find a way to sneak away from those long tables plagued by predictable conversations, dirty looks, and misunderstandings when settling the check. As soon as she arrived in a new city, she'd find as quickly as possible a good spot near her hotel to get street food, and she'd eat there as often as she could, far away from her gourmet colleagues. Those she now has sitting at her table are not very different from those others: they complain, get excited, swap information, invent, make assumptions, are overwhelmed by the excessive burden of their own jobs while at the same time envy the jobs of others. At some point they mention the exhibition-homage, but they don't add anything new. Mara's mind returns to her encounter with Talvikki and the other bits of information she found that night on the computer at that hotel. She tries to memorize the five most important bits in order to have them on hand tomorrow, when she goes to visit her, when she goes to see the work that Tal spoke to her about at such length throughout that long night they waited together. She's certain that once she's there, in the taxidermist's house, the name of one of the components will pop up in front of her eyes. Maybe they'll be the same ones Tal herself uses in her experiments with dissolved animal remains. Very likely they're the same, she's convinced, but she is eager to finally confirm it. She has to keep her cool, it's obvious that luck is on her side. Only one more day. No, less than twenty-four hours, she sees when she looks at one of the walls where the tarnished clock, always somewhere in those common spaces, is hanging.

• • •

At this point he shouldn't let her cross the threshold, the taxidermist says in greeting as soon as he hears her open the door to his cabinet. The horses are like brides, they shouldn't be seen once they are ready for the ceremony. They're resplendent, Mara sees, not without a certain pang. She puts on her best room-guard expression and says that she's willing to leave whenever he'd like her to. The taxidermist swings his whole body around to look at her. With rage, with disdain, it seems to her, as if her comment were impertinent. Then he immerses himself once again in something that he seems to be obsessing about on Mancha's left temple. They'll emerge when it's time, he says. This shadow always hovers at the end, this threat of having betrayed the original. Always at the end, like a trial by fire. He asks her to hand him the portraits. Mara hands him the file that contains the only reproductions that her boss deemed valid when he started his work: two are photos taken during the celebrated journey and the third is a watercolor by a traditionalist painter who was fairly well known in his era. When he was young he drew a lot, he says. He couldn't wait until the teachers at school and his parents would leave him alone to draw in peace. But he was never interested in inventing, he always worked from a model. He would choose it, prepare it, then hold it in his mind, and then he'd let the pencil do its thing. Already then the only thing he wanted to do was return to the original, as far as he's concerned his work is a return trip. This has made him very perceptive in guessing people's pasts. And he doesn't know exactly why, but if he had to taxidermy her, Mara, he wouldn't find inspiration in a museum guard. Maybe she can explain why, he says, and turns to look at her. She answers with the first cliché that pops into her head, though she has to admit that her surprise detracted from her precision. She can't avoid a certain nervousness. Nor must she forget one of the types of silence, the sixth: "A stupid silence is when the tongue is stilled and the spirit numb, and the entire person appears to be so deeply taciturn that it means nothing." She wonders if she talked too much during her walk with Tal, if everything will be ruined right when she's ready to take the pivotal step. She wonders how she can feel panic now, right now, right here. She needs to remind herself what she was capable of: in comparison to the previous sabotage, this is child's play; or it should be. She sits on her assistant's stool and tries to calm down. She opens her mouth to say that she forgot something, she'll be right back, but at the same instant her boss looks at her, enlightened, as if he'd resolved the problem with the horse's temple that had obsessed him, or as if the temple had offered him a truce, and then he tells her that now, right now, they're going to go to his house where Talvikki Ranta is waiting for them.

• • •

They're sitting on the ground, shielded by the trees in the park. It seems like an excess of caution to Ringo, who reminds her that they didn't sign on for an Indiana Jones escapade, but Mara orders him to not move a muscle until she tells him to. The night is mild, a peaceful summer night, which seems to her to be a good omen. A group of totally self-absorbed teenagers walk by. Perfect, nobody should see them there. Mara made sure to find one of the least transited spots for this obligatory wait. The sleeping pill will take effect in forty minutes, the pharmacist said, and that's what they're waiting for. This isn't so hard, or at least less hard than the previous step, the barbecue she just shared with the security folks and that she'd imagined would be simpler, or less uncomfortable. Maybe because by this time she has really started to like them. The exact dose at exactly the right time, the pharmacist repeated, with a kind of visionary certainty that combined the licensed professional and the witch doctor. She remembers her long fingernails, painted a metallic color, and the way she moved them to emphasize her words. Moreover, it's very important to take the personality of the patient into account, she added, a piece of information to which Mara paid particularly close attention. At first she thought that since the more introverted of the security guards sleeps there, in the guard house, where they just had the barbecue, his dose should be lower, but after that warning she thought that his organism would absorb the sleeping pill with the same reticence as he absorbs everything going on around him, so she settled on identical doses for both. There, waiting in the shadows and under the strict order of silence that she imposed on herself and Ringo, she has only that to mull over, the conversation with the pharmacist. Or to imagine what her friends in security might be doing minute by minute, at what point in their nightly routine they will succumb to a deep slumber, but something blurry between sorrow and pride dissuades her from continuing down that path. Infallible, the pharmacist repeated, accompanied by a metallic bang on the top of the bottle. Mara had made sure to look for someone far away in space and time so that her purchase would not raise the slightest suspicion. Ringo had been a great help in this, as well: he remembered that woman, that goddess and provider of unmarked blister packs, thanks to which he had managed to survive the last three summers with his family, and he also drove Mara to that small town in the mountains. She looks at her watch; still fifteen minutes to go. Something that puts you to sleep and the next day you perceive as nothing more than a deeper sleep than usual, that's all, that's what Mara asked for before inventing a very complicated story the pharmacist did not pay the least attention to, as if it were common practice to put somebody else to sleep. Age of patient, weight, required hours of unconsciousness, she asked; she seemed to be following a protocol long established by some powerful government agency. Mara looks at her watch again and jumps up. With Ringo walking about ten steps behind her, just as they had practiced, they reach the guard house. Also as planned, she enters through the bathroom window and walks over to the wall where the keys to the rooms and workshops are hanging. She puts the one to the taxidermy cabinet in her pocket and stealthily walks back to the window. After an initial sense of relief, she is now worried that she didn't see the security guard passed out on the way. She stands there paralyzed for a few minutes, to see if she hears anything, or to recover from the nervousness she didn't expect. Nothing. She would get on her knees and kiss those silver-painted nails, she thinks, as she jumps into the park out of the same window she entered. She motions to Ringo. The next step seems simpler to her: she knows the workshop perfectly and, as far as she knows, there is no possibility that a taxidermied horse will trot away in the middle of the night.

• • •

From the *Notebook*:
"We feel proud to be a National Race, the only one born and bred in this land and by us, the only one to be found through-

out our nation, contributing day in and day out to the flourishing of our livestock. It is the only race that can survive the conditions on the Patagonian steppes, in the Chaqueña jungle, in the dry and arid North, and throughout the Iberá Wetlands. This same one that crosses the vast distances of the Pampas, and the same one that neighs proudly throughout all of America."

(From the brochure of the Association of Criollo Horse Breeders, Buenos Aires, circa 2012.)

• • •

At the last minute, the lawyer decided not to speak. His name appears as one of the speakers on the program they printed for this long-awaited opening of the exhibition, but he has now retreated, his jaws tenser than ever, as he watches the public relations person for the Association. The young man is doing his job impeccably well, Mara admits. Not even two hours have passed since the workmen opened the doors and discovered that the emblematic horses were in ruins, a bloated mess, in even worse shape than they had been in before this last taxidermy, worse than they'd ever been, and he's now performing a high-wire act in order to keep to the same speech he'd prepared for this great homage, even though the subjects of the homage aren't here. Or rather, they are, but they're unrecognizable. That was the exact word the museum director used when she found herself obliged to mention the subject in her introductory remarks. Afterwards, she skillfully insisted on how paradoxical it was that precisely as a result of this lamentable and surely temporary impossibility to exhibit Mancha and Gato on this day and at this time, the horses were more present than ever to this lovely audience gathered here today, which showed how deeply they have permeated our collective memory and the hearts of each and every person, and at the same time how this flings open the doors of the future to new specimens of the breed, who were also there with them on this gorgeous sunny day. And she went on in that vein. Now, while somebody is talking over the loudspeakers to remind the audience what time the horses the Association brought for the homage will begin to participate in the equestrian events, the director gives the microphone to the taxidermist and assures the audience that he, as a specialist, will be able to give a concise report about what happened and even venture certain strategies for the future of Mancha and Gato, who will surely soon once again be what they once were. He takes the microphone in a state of evident shock and clears his throat. He's livid, shrunken, much more distressed than his pieces. He opens his mouth, as if he is finally going to say something, but he only clears his throat again. His silence does not provoke in the audience the curiosity that's described in Mara's manual of rhetoric, an increased interest from the sudden absence of word and movement, as described in her favorite passage, but instead creates a charmless void wherein everybody's attention turns to the goings on in the plaza: children running, street vendors hawking, riders and grooms preparing the horses for the equestrian events. It could almost be said that nobody besides the organizers seems very upset over the absence of the famous horses. On stage, the taxidermist keeps struggling and finally manages to stammer out a sentence that seems to make reference to a chemical attack. He hesitates before each word, as if his discomfort and the need to find the appropriate euphemism overwhelm him, as if he were overwhelmed by sorrow. He indicates that in the next few days specialists will come from the university to determine the specifics of this attack, which has clear signs of terrorism, and then he begins another sentence that he doesn't manage to finish. He stares at a distant spot in space, like those actors who are suddenly overwhelmed by stage fright because of a line they can't remember. Mara is certain that he knows perfectly well what destroyed the horses. She has no doubt that when he touched that gelatinous mass the hides had become, he knew exactly what had caused it. Even the few people who seemed interested in his speech begin to wander away. The sun is increasingly intense, and this must remind them of the number of activities that have already started without them. The function continues, because the director was very clear in her decision to not allow any changes to the opening program. Now a breeder of Criollo horses is speaking, or the owner of a pharmaceutical company where they clone horses like these, or both at the same time, Mara doesn't manage to understand though she does perceive the lack of subtlety with which the speaker invites the listeners to focus on what he calls future options. Or something like that. The taxidermist stands there, not even daring to leave the stage.

• • •

From the *Notebook*:
"A breed is born and persists in the market for as long as it efficiently meets a need. The breeders of Criollo horses have had the enormous virtue, throughout the years, of constantly selecting for the demands of the market. In the nineteen for-

ties they developed a short, compact biotype with a solid frame and a back of steel in order to meet the demands of intense cattle ranching throughout the country, producing stallions fit for widespread interbreeding with general biotypes. Its strength also allowed it to fill the need for draft horses, necessary for transportation at that time. Time and mechanization led to the need for a lighter biotype, almost exclusively suited for riding and, through selective breeding, a taller and more agile profile emerged. Entering the market as a horse suited for recreational activities was an enormous challenge for the Criollo. The range of competitive equestrian games allowed for selection for docility, agility, strength, courage, speed, and total obedience to the rider. Today we are firmly embarked on that path and fully solvent, working day in and day out and investing our time and capital to adapt, once more, to the market in order to guarantee our survival."

(From the brochure of the Association of Criollo Horse Breeders, Buenos Aires, circa 2012.)

• • •

Mara tries to find Talvikki among the dwindling audience, but nothing, not a trace, which worries her; she knows that the course things take will depend on her reaction, in part. She wonders if she's already heard about what happened to the horses, or if she is shut away in her house, wearing an astronaut suit, absorbed in her remains and her toxic materials. That afternoon when Mara went to visit her, supposedly in order to see her work, she managed to get her husband rather than her to expound upon the ways the chemicals Tal works with decompose his discards in different ways. He even stopped to comment on specific pieces, somewhere between disturbed and enchanted by the kinds of transformations they bore witness to. Mara wonders if the taxidermist would really be capable of suspecting his wife. That day, she took the opportunity to ask him more than a few questions, and he answered all of them, fundamentally those related to the decomposition of fur and hides. Maybe some of the materials Talvikki uses are the same that he uses, maybe not. How to know with a boss who always made sure to camouflage his solutions. That day, she remembers, Talvikki listened to everything as if she were merely another embalmed piece; it was difficult for Mara to reconcile that image with the woman she'd met at the station, with the artist spoken about on innumerable websites. On the other hand, it wasn't difficult at all for her to stuff a couple of flasks in her backpack without anybody seeing.

• • •

From the *Notebook:*

Some common ground between embalmed and taxidermied pieces: the meticulousness, the perfect composure. A tribute for posterity. The soothing encapsulation of memories. Good manners perpetrated ad infinitum. Embellishments, trophies, fetishism. Pride. Fears appeased, the void abolished. The fantasy of subduing not only the dead, but death itself. Nevertheless, all of these facets are abolished in Fragonard's figures. Not only abolished: banished, subverted, even ironized. Fragonard's technique: to flay cadavers—of animals and humans—and inject a metal alloy into the arteries to solidify them. Something like that. I don't know much else, apparently there's not much else to know: Fragonard and another secret carried to the grave. What is known, what can be seen in the few pieces that survive in the museum outside Paris, is the terrifying dimension he was able to give to his technique. Embalming as a corrosive critique, a devastating mockery. It's difficult to get those figures out of your mind, your retina. More than figures: visions. More than visions: nightmares. The gaze, the madness of "Buste d'homme." The devastating laughter of "Le cavalier," his most famous piece. It's difficult to look at that piece. To see it, see it in the most literal and all-encompassing sense of the word, look straight at the perverse smile he placed in this world for us. Not a divinity or a huge explosion but rather a smile, a smile like the one on the flayed figures of Fragonard. In the middle of Illuminism, a smile of outrage. According to a website that quickly vanished, the human figure in that work is Fragonard's beloved, who committed suicide when her family forbade them from marrying. Anybody would think it is the cadaver of a man, and the museum asserts that it is, but according to the vanished website it was a woman. Fragonard's beloved, to be more precise. Not a trace of this, in any case. Museums and their publishing machinery. This piece, "Le cavalier," for example, is exhibited mutilated: only the rider—the Amazon suicide?—on the horse. Missing are the other pieces that, in Fragonard's original version—in his theatrical version, in the pieces he liked to assemble—accompanied the rider/Amazon on her last, triumphal ride: an entourage consisting of embalmed horses and human fetuses riding on rams. I look in the dictionary to confirm that "carnero" is a kind of sheep, and the definition reminds me that in addition to meaning "ram," it also means the place where they throw dead bodies.

(After a visit to the museum of l'École nationale vétérinaire, Masions-Alfort, France, 2013.)

• • •

She still can't find Talvikki among the crowd but she does find the director, who is walking toward her and intercepts her. The lawyer also approaches with a grave expression on his face. To think that you took care of them so well for so many months, the director says, and she places her hand on Mara's shoulder. Now, because of her boss's breakdown, she has to ask her a favor, a very special favor: to accompany the lawyer to the cabinet where the horses are. Or what's left of them, she says, glancing fleetingly at the floor. She'll wait for him afterwards in her office, she tells the lawyer when she lifts her head, then starts to walk away. But she takes two steps and stops. She calls to Mara with an interjection because her name escapes her or she never knew it and tells her to take as many photos as necessary, as many as the lawyer asks her to. This business of returning so soon to what is called in a detective novel the scene of the crime causes Mara a certain amount of grief; she also is afraid of running into one of her guard friends so soon, but she admits to herself that she is trapped. She walks dutifully and without speaking, as is fitting to her status as a museum guard turned guide. The cabinet: the usual semidarkness. She let's the lawyer enter first. Before entering, he arranges his poncho, which now, without horses and without an exhibition, looks even phonier than before. Then, when they approach the pieces, Mara confirms how perfect, how irremediable, the attack has been. Their backs look like they were ridden by the Devil himself. She imagined a different effect, something more gelatinous, something very different from this scorching, these black gashes, these marks of having been pulled too late out of a fire. She looks out of the corner of her eye at the lawyer, who is livid. Even in the semidarkness, ostensibly livid. Mara approaches the taxidermist's table and pretends to be straightening things up, as if she were carrying on with her habitual tasks in spite of everything, as if her modesty prevented her from bearing witness to this scene. The lawyer takes out his cell phone and calls the taxidermist. He wants an explanation, an idea, any idea, but above all, an explanation. He knows he's in a state of shock, of course, but he also knows how he works, who he is. He is not at all convinced by the museum director's explanation. That he made a mistake with the chemicals he used; impossible. That pencil-pusher is trying to incriminate him, destroy his career, dodge the problem, but she's not going to get anywhere with such an absurd theory. What's his explanation for what happened, that's what he wants to know? Now, right now. He doesn't care about his state of shock, this can't wait till he sees him. Now. This is going to cause serious problems, as he knows. Not to mention losses. Until that moment he'd thought that the taxidermist understood much more clearly that this restoration and the first clone will swing open the doors to a multi-million dollar market. Multi-million. He can't pretend he doesn't understand, he's been a member of the Association for a long time, even longer than him. He thought the taxidermist clearly understood the symbolic importance of his work, the symbolic power of those horses that now aren't horses and aren't anything. He needs an explanation, now. Now. The December heat can be felt inside the cabinet. The lawyer takes off his poncho with a surprising lack of elegance and is finally quiet, listening to what the taxidermist is telling him. His jaws are tighter than ever, it seems that what he is hearing from the other end of the line is making him even more upset. He interrupts and tells the taxidermist that if he is not willing to see it with his own eyes, then he will have to tell him: there is no doubt at all that this is the work of his wife, his crazy wife and her obsessions, sticking her nose into what he does, into those dead bodies that are no good for anything. How many times has he told him that he married a madwoman, how many?

• • •

The buzzing of rumors can still be heard up and down the hallways of the museum. It's already been a week and they haven't gone down even one decibel; on the contrary, they've gotten louder and moved in even more unexpected directions and incorporated fantastical elements. They're being fed to a large extent on what the newspapers as well as the local and national radio stations are saying about the incident. Three days ago the director called an emergency meeting and forbade all employees from making any statements until justice had been done, but Mara hears from Luisa about the tricks her colleagues are using to leak information. They just happen to run into a reporter in the bakery or in line at the bank, they just happen to have a journalist among their online friends. Thanks to these spontaneous acts, they throw into disarray the communication strategies of the Association and its members, of whom there are many. From her seat, finally recuperated, Mara no longer hears them, neither the ones nor the others; the serenity her sabotage has given her is inversely proportional to the general chaos. She managed to rid herself of interruptions and take revenge on the characters who embodied them, she is firmly in her rights to finish her hiatus in peace before returning to her experiment. As the afternoon heat enters, attenuated by the high ceiling, she is happy she chose this place. She finds that the lumbar contact functions perfectly; she is certain that she will begin without much effort to reintroduce the protocol of her experiment in detachment, it will simply happen on its own. If she knew the techniques for talking to horses that she recently saw in a documentary, she would go into the locked cabinet and whisper in their ears how grateful she is to them, how beautiful they are, in all their ruin. The only consequence she regrets concerns Talvikki, about whom nothing has been heard since the day of the sabotage. Nothing. Not at the museum and not on the internet; she checked. And not anywhere else, Luisa assures her. She seems to have been swallowed by the Earth.

• • •

From the *Notebook*:

At the end of the twentieth century, an English scientist studies telepathic phenomena and other forms of extraordinary communication between some people and some animals. When he talks about horses, he mentions the abilities of so-called horse-whisperers, among whom an Irishman named Daniel Sullivan was a pioneer. He would approach the wildest horses and manage to tame them as if by magic. He seemed to talk to them, his contemporaries said. The only thing he said was that a gypsy had taught him. But one day in 1810, when he was already called Daniel Horse-Whisperer Sullivan, the Irishman died and carried his secret to the grave. The secret formula, the secret method (the return of the secret: an anachronism in the age of the end of privacy). On the other hand, one of those who carried on his work, John Solomon Rarey, a boy from Ohio who became famous for taming the most untamable horses without resorting to any form of violence, described in minute detail his own method and published a book in 1862 with a predictable title. Emerson admired him, seeing him in some way as a revolutionary. I suppose Thoreau did as well. The revealing details don't matter here; what does matter is the fact that his method was simple, silent, and solitary. No bombast, no diatribe.

(After Rupert Sheldrake, *Dogs that Know When their Owners Are Coming Home: And Other Unexplained Powers of Animals*, London: Hutchinson, 1999.)

• • •

As soon as she steps outside, Luisa tells her that her aunt decided to join them for lunch, it was impossible to say no, she knows how she is. The detachment that Mara is so sure she has been recovering over the last few days is suddenly threatened by these words. She says nothing, they keep walking. They are still at that time of year when crossing the plaza under the noonday sun reminds her of a trek across the desert. Inside, Mara is grateful for the certainty that by next summer she will be in a different place. She doesn't know where, but definitely somewhere else. Honoria is already there when they arrive, at a table, not the one she and Luisa usually choose on Fridays. She is wearing dark glasses: without them she can't go out in the glare of January, she says. She wants to know if Mara is satisfied with her plan, with the direction things took. She doesn't beat at all around the bush, as Mara predicted. Fortunately, the waiter interrupts them. Mara asks a couple of questions about the items on the menu she already knows by heart. Then she finds a way to say that she hadn't thought about it in those terms, not in terms of results. She can't think of any other strategy to avoid what will follow, nor does she know if what follows is a threat of being exposed or a new humbling lecture. She thinks she prefers the first. Luisa makes a comment in an attempt to change the direction of the conversation, but she fails. It's a pity, a big fat pity, Honoria says. She thought that Mara had listened to her, had understood her that day. That she would have known how to wait, as she advised her. Wait and organize. That she would have avoided wasting her indignation and unease, her revolutionary energy. But no, she was wrong. Mara was wrong and she herself was wrong to have believed that she'd finally found someone in this place she could work with to rebuild a movement, an efficient organization. Mara doesn't know, Honoria continues, the extent to which she could have counted on her if she'd listened to her, the extent to which she would have contributed to her struggle, not only against the taxidermist but also against every single traditionalist and reactionary front that gathers in this town, those enemy strongholds against which her husband did battle his entire life. But she couldn't, she has to abstain, because no worthy battle can be waged in collaboration with an isolated act, an act that is without a doubt nothing more than an expression of decadence, a childhood malady.

• • •

From her happily recuperated chair, Mara observes the pieces in the room and notices that she no longer cleans them very well, though nobody else seems to have noticed. Things have come together so well that they don't even notice her anymore. In the last two months she has almost not had to utter a word, it still surprises her how easily one can manage in this world on the basis of a handful of onomatopoeias and affirmations. These last, often only corporal. They work perfectly. That's all that's needed for them not to interrupt her, allowing her to sink deeper and deeper into her lumbar contact, the drifting of her mind. She didn't even get back to her experiment in the garden. The truth is she doesn't miss it, she hasn't even looked closely enough to see what's growing, to try to see if there is a difference between the species that she planted and the weeds. She doesn't miss it at all. More recently, she has instead been focusing on her next chapter, her next act that will go against the grain. She never imagined the effect Honoria's baroque accusations would have on her. What she had at first heard as an obsolete discourse has shown her, in the last few months of her return to detachment, another vision, a new perspective: her flights from the redundancies of the world transformed into solitary resistance. From revulsion to anarchism, not bad. She still doesn't know if she will keep that perspective in mind only to use as an alibi in a court of law, or if she will incorporate it into the theoretical framework of her future escapades. There will be time to think about that. For now, she is interested only in rereading Talvikki's letter. Sent from Italy under a false name to the museum. When they handed her the envelope she had the impression, for a split second, that someone from her old life might have managed to find her, but no. It is terrifyingly reassuring to discover how easy it is to dispense with the surroundings that at some point seemed to be so omnipresent, so inexorable. Talvikki says that she simply wants to thank her. If Mara had not destroyed the horses, she would still be there, wondering how and when she could leave. Her Gauguin-among-the-savages period had ended long before, she knew it all too well, long before the two of them met, but she hadn't found a way to end it, hadn't found a ritual to bid farewell. Until Mara managed to steal that compound she was using, and then things took their own course. Unexpected, really. That afternoon, when she saw her hide the bottle in her backpack, she thought that her work had inspired her, and that perhaps she wanted to experiment with BioArt in her spare time. She has to admit that Mara managed to surprise her. The truth is that to this day she cannot figure out why she did it, though she doesn't care, much less now that her lawyer has taken charge of the problem. She just wants to thank her, she repeats. She moved to Italy, a country where she always wanted to spend some time. If she's ever in the neighborhood, she should not hesitate to get in touch with her. Then, the closing formalities.

MARÍA SONIA CRISTOFF (Trelew, Patagonia, 1965) is the author of five works of fiction and nonfiction, including *False Calm* and *Include Me Out*, and lives in Buenos Aires, where she teaches creative writing. Her journalism can be found in *Neue Zürcher Zeitung*, *Perfil*, and *La Nación*. She has edited volumes on literary nonfiction (*Idea crónica* and *Pasaje a Oriente*) and participated in a series of collective works. Her work has been translated into six languages.

KATHERINE SILVER is an award-winning literary translator and the former director of the Banff International Literary Translation Centre (BILTC). Her most recent and forthcoming translations include works by César Aira, Julio Cortázar, Juan Carlos Onetti, and Julio Ramón Ribeyro. She is the author of *Echo Under Story* (What Books Press, 2019) and does volunteer interpreting for asylum seekers.

Transit Books is a nonprofit publisher of international and American literature, based in Oakland, California. Founded in 2015, Transit Books is committed to the discovery and promotion of enduring works that carry readers across borders and communities. Visit us online to learn more about our forthcoming titles, events, and opportunities to support our mission.

TRANSITBOOKS.ORG